"You should try to rest."

"What about you? You need rest, too."

"Nope. FBI agents don't sleep. Didn't you know?" Derek offered a smile, but even in the faint glow of the fluorescent lights, Hannah could see how weary he was.

"I keep thinking that this is just not the day I thought it was going to be. All I wanted to do was go to work, get some great experience that might lead to a permanent position after law school, then go home and read a novel. And now? Now I've been shot at— how many times?"

"I'm sure it's been a little confusing for you, especially with the news I had to bring to you."

"So this is going to be your life now, as an FBI agent? Always on the run?"

"Some parts of the job will probably be boring, but there's also sure to be more of this."

"More girls that need your protection?" Where did that come from? He had been hers at one point in time, but not anymore.

By sixth grade, **Meghan Carver** knew she wanted to write. After a degree in English from Millikin University, she detoured to law school, completing a juris doctorate from Indiana University. She then worked in immigration law and taught college-level composition. Now she homeschools her six children with her husband. When she isn't writing, homeschooling or planning another travel adventure, she is active in her church, sews and reads.

Books by Meghan Carver

Love Inspired Suspense

Under Duress
Deadly Disclosure

DEADLY DISCLOSURE

MEGHAN CARVER

HARLEQUIN® LOVE INSPIRED® SUSPENSE

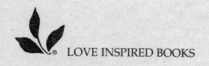 **LOVE INSPIRED BOOKS**

Recycling programs
for this product may
not exist in your area.

ISBN-13: 978-0-373-67844-0

Deadly Disclosure

Copyright © 2017 by Meghan Carver

www.Harlequin.com

Printed in U.S.A.

For you did not receive the Spirit of bondage again to fear, but you received the Spirit of adoption by whom we cry out, "Abba, Father."
—*Romans* 8:15

To my parents, both adoptive and biological.

ONE

Hannah McClarnon's low heels click-clacked a rapid tempo on the cement. Her heart beat out a similar staccato as the black truck revved its engine behind her.

She stepped up her pace to get across the street to what she hoped would be the safety of the sidewalk, sneaking a peek at the driver out of her peripheral vision. Sunglasses shoved up tight on his face to block out the late afternoon sun hid any distinguishing features.

In a flash of the sunlight off of the truck's side-view mirror, the driver hit the accelerator. The truck bore down on her at an increasing speed. Hannah's heart seized in her chest as she clutched her tote and dashed to the sidewalk. An alley appeared a few feet down, and as she ran for safety, a *crack* tore the air. The brick next to her arm exploded with the bullet. A squeal escaped from somewhere deep inside of her, and she rushed into the protective enclosure of the alleyway.

Hannah leaned against the brick wall, gulping air. Was she safe or was the assailant still there? A quick glance down the alley only revealed a turn. Which way did it go? Or was it a dead end? She hadn't worked in the little downtown area long enough to have had the opportunity to explore all the nooks and crannies yet. At least the alley was too narrow for the truck.

The clock on her phone warned her that she had less than ten minutes until her next appointment, something mysterious that her new boss, Mallory Callahan, had scheduled. She quickly dialed 911 and relayed her emergency to dispatch. But could she wait that long until help arrived? Although she couldn't fathom why the man in the truck had shot at her, neither did she have any reason to believe that he would just drive away.

Of course, she'd been in the public eye before. She was the only daughter of shoe-manufacturing magnate Willford McClarnon. This was Heartwood Hill, though, a suburb of Indianapolis, and it was a bit unusual since her father's business was in

Lafayette. And this guy obviously hadn't been looking at her shoes.

With trembling hands, Hannah tapped the camera icon and then hit the reverse button. The urge to peek around the corner pressed hard, but she forced it away. Grasping the end of her phone with her fingertips, she slid the camera end of the phone past the corner of the building. As soon as the screen showed a wide angle of the street, she snapped the photo and brought the phone back toward her.

She took a deep breath and examined the picture.

The truck was still there, a black monstrous thing with a star-shaped decal in the front windshield. No one else was around. There was no one on the sidewalk, and no vehicular traffic filled the street, but that was not unusual for so late in the afternoon. Office hours had ended a while ago, and the professional district had mostly emptied as everyone headed for home.

Now what?

Her destination, the three-story building where the Callahan twins had their law offices, was just around the corner, but would the alley connect? If it did, she could be there, safe in her cubical, in a few minutes. Perhaps law enforcement would arrive by that time.

The truck revved again, and perspiration slicked her palms so that she nearly dropped her phone. Apparently, the shooter thought she was an easy target and could just lie in wait for her to reappear, like a mouse emerging from its hole. Well, Hannah McClarnon was no mouse. She wouldn't stay here and wait for another bullet.

Instead, she straightened her back against the brick wall and began inching down the alley. By the time she reached the corner, she couldn't see the street. That should mean that the man in the truck couldn't see her, but she couldn't stop herself from hurrying across the chasm. She dodged a couple of trash cans and a pile of pallets. Around another corner, the alley opened up just across the two-lane street from the parking lot in front of the office building.

Returning her phone to her tote, she briefly pressed her hand to her heart before gripping the bag. With a quick glance up and down the street, she forced herself to step out from what felt like the safety of the brick enclosure. "Lord, keep me safe," she prayed, as she puffed hair off her forehead. Her whispering voice sounded loud as it whooshed in her ears.

As she was about to step up onto the curb on the opposite side of the street, the squeal of tires on asphalt startled her. She pumped her legs into a jog, gripping the handles of her handbag so tightly her fingers went white. Suddenly, the professional image she had tried so hard to exude in her first real job didn't matter. Dread crept up her spine at a breakneck pace. A glance to her right revealed it was the same truck again. He had found her. The man in the truck with the star-shaped decal.

Hannah felt her stomach lurch, bile rising in her throat.

The roar of his engine warned her that he was approaching again. He had to be only a few yards behind her. She quickened her pace and inhaled deeply for a quick shot of energy. It was doubtful that anyone from the office building would see her and come to her rescue. Most likely, at this late hour, only the Callahans were left, and only one of their windows, the one at the end of a hallway, faced the parking lot.

Where were those sirens she had summoned with her emergency call?

Perhaps she had an advantage, being on foot. A landscaped flower bed with evenly spaced brick posts ran between the street and the parking lot. The turn-in for vehicles was around the corner. Ignoring the dampness of the grass and mulch on her new pumps and stocking feet, she hopped between a couple of bushes and onto the asphalt parking lot.

All she could think to do was keep walking. Quickly. She kept herself as concealed by the decorative brick posts as possible.

Her phone trilled from the front pocket of her bag. The sudden noise reverberated through her, and in her half-panicked state of mind, she sped up her stride. She let the phone ring, and it sounded like a gong counting out her final steps.

Hannah glanced at the truck, still approaching. Was he trying to get closer for a clean shot? It seemed as if those posts were successfully blocking her. The ringing stopped, the sudden silence urging her on.

The truck roared around the corner to the entrance to the parking lot, gone from her sight, albeit only temporarily. Perhaps she could get inside before he pulled into the lot.

She murmured another prayer—*Lord, get me inside safely*—and clutched her tote. Her lunch break had been much later than usual, more of an early supper, and shadows were just beginning to gather as the sun sank lower in the sky. The trees that stood in stately rows in front of the building seemed to snake out clutching arms, and she shook her head to clear the wanderings of her imagination.

Woman, pull yourself together. This is no way for a future Juris Doctor to behave. One more year until graduation, and then she hoped, she prayed, that she had a bright future ahead.

Only a couple of other vehicles sat in the lot, and they were empty.

She glanced up at the granite that shone pink in the evening sun. The artificial light from the offices of the upper floor spilled out to the side of the building and battled with the sunshine, an eerie illumination that skittered a chill up her arms. Safety was up there, just a few steps away. She tightened the belt on her black cardigan and tried to square her shoulders as she rushed toward the door. The black truck careened around the corner and paused at the entrance of the parking lot, as if the driver was assessing the situation and possible risks. Then it turned into the lot.

Alarm shook Hannah, goose bumps popping out on her forearms. Still looking back at the truck, she lengthened her strides toward the door, clutching her bag as a shield. If she made it to safety, she might laugh later about the absurdity of a little bit of canvas and a coin purse protecting her from the weapon that the menace in the truck wielded against her.

She approached the front of the building at a half run, sensing as much as hearing the passenger-side window of the truck power down. Her hand on the door handle, her eyes closed to whatever danger might be coming, she heard the door open and a firm hand gripped her bicep. A scream stuck in her throat as a shot fired. The hand pulled her inside and down to the floor as bits of granite rained on the walk in front of the door. She landed on her knees on the cool marble floor.

"Over there." A husky male voice commanded her to crawl in the direction he pointed, to the side away from the door. He stood in front of her, shielding her with his body.

She clutched her bag, gulping air, willing her breathing to slow to a normal rate. Was she safe now?

"Are you okay?" Her rescuer turned toward her.

Hannah was met with rich, dark chocolate eyes, an intense gaze that summoned a wave of recognition and an attraction she had thought was long dead. "Derek?"

He watched the truck turn in a circle, surveying the area, then angle toward the door. The driver-side window lowered. Derek Chambers kept his SIG Sauer down but ready.

In his peripheral vision, he saw Hannah rotate and begin to stand. He held a hand out to stop her. "Yes, it's me. Stay down for now. Against the wall."

She complied. "Who's out there?"

"We'll get to that in a minute. I'm your six-o'clock appointment, but let me resolve this situation first." He'd been sent with some specific information to give her, but now was not the time for that conversation. Not with a shooter outside. The faint wail of sirens drifted in the door. "Did you call 911 already?"

The truck engine revved, and Derek stole a glance her way to see Hannah pull her purse close as she struggled to maintain a neutral expression. "Yes. Several minutes ago. Now who is that guy?"

An excellent question, but first... "Are you all right? The bullet struck the side of the building, but I think I got you inside before the granite shattered. What about your hands and knees?" He let his gaze sweep the street and the parking lot. The guy in the truck had certainly chosen the right time to make his move. The professional district of little Heartwood Hill was deserted at this hour.

Derek heard Hannah rub her hands together. "I'm a little sore, but I'll be okay thanks to you." A second glance revealed she was stretching her shoulders. "This isn't the first time he's shot at me. He blew a big chunk of brick off a building a block or so over. I think my bigger problem is that man in the truck."

"Yes. I heard the shot and was on my way to help you." He could have gone straight up to the offices when he arrived for the appointment, but he hadn't wanted their first encounter after so many years to be in the presence of her employer. Waiting for her in the lobby had seemed like the best plan.

A gun barrel appeared in the window of the truck. Derek's senses rushed to full alert. He raised his weapon and aimed at the driver-side door as he maneuvered behind the granite exterior wall of the office building as much as the structure and his bulk would allow.

Before he could decide whether to shoot out a tire, the wall exploded next to Derek. The shot missed him and Hannah, who was well-covered, but a second pockmark now marred the building. A couple of cars sped past on the main road, and the truck peeled out of the parking lot, raising the window as it went.

That last one was a warning shot, especially with the sirens rapidly approaching, and Derek got the message loud and clear. The shooter would be back. That was fine with Derek. He would still be protecting Hannah, whether she welcomed it or not.

He holstered his SIG and inhaled deeply, willing his heart to stop racing. But the fervent beat of his pulse only briefly slowed, because then he turned and helped the beautiful woman he'd just rescued to her feet. He put his hands on her upper arms and held her, a warm, comfortable feeling that summoned up pleasant memories of the past that trickled through him...for a nanosecond. A look of surprise and dismay flitted across her face like spring storm clouds and acted as a splash of cold rain on him. He had a job to do, and he was determined to do it well. The FBI would not be disappointed in him, a new academy graduate. Derek pushed her away, out of sight of the door and nearby window, reminding himself that it was also best to push her out of his mind. There was one task to do here, and it didn't involve dredging up old feelings from the past. Judging by the arch of her eyebrows and the pinch of her mouth as she studied him, he wouldn't have any problem keeping himself detached.

But the tiny lines around her pretty brown eyes softened as she considered him. She had matured into a lovely, self-confident woman, and there didn't seem to be any remnant of the awkwardness of her teen years. Her petite frame stood a few inches shorter than him, and her soft brown hair fell over her trembling shoulders as she looked up at him. "What do you mean you got here just in time? Does this have something to do with my appointment?"

As the adrenaline of the rescue subsided, a subtle scent of flowers began to tickle his nose, probably from Hannah. He retrieved his badge and showed it to her. "I'm with the

FBI now. I've been sent with some information that directly affects you." He averted his gaze. If only he had a script, then he might sound suave and confident. Desperation welled up as he struggled for words to comfort the stricken woman standing before him. The sirens screamed down the street and advanced to the parking lot, saving him from further discussion, at least for the time being. "I need to talk to the police first, but then let's talk privately. That's why I made the appointment."

"Sure. Upstairs. My cubical."

The elevator dinged its arrival, and Reid Palmer, Derek's friend from their prior days together on the Heartwood Hill police force emerged. He hurried to Derek and shook his hand, nodding briefly to Hannah. "Everyone okay? I heard the shots from upstairs."

"Yeah." He nodded toward the parking lot, where a couple of cruisers, lights flashing, had pulled in. "Help has arrived."

Reid stepped forward to the officers, but Derek turned back to Hannah. "You'll have to talk to the officers and tell them what happened. Are you all right? Can you do that?"

She nodded, a look of trepidation spreading across her face. "Will you stay with me?"

Her hands still shook as she brushed a lock of hair off her forehead. Being shot at was not terribly new to Derek, but it must have been terrifying for her.

"I'm not going anywhere." Derek suppressed a sigh as the adrenaline faded from his system. He longed to gulp deep breaths of oxygen to refuel, but he wanted to appear calm and steady for Hannah's sake. He forced a grin and lightly touched the back of her arm to turn her toward the officers. "Let's get this done."

A half hour later, the officers were clued into everything that had just transpired and had a copy of the photo Hannah had snapped of the truck. Now, the hardest part of his assignment had arrived. "Time to talk?" he asked her.

She checked her wristwatch and shuffled her purse again with trembling hands. "Sure." Hesitating all of a sudden, she peered around Derek and out the front door. "He's gone for certain now, though, isn't he?"

"With all this law enforcement? Definitely." At least, he should be if he was as clever a villain as the FBI suspected.

She turned toward the bank of elevators and nodded for him to follow, her steps short as if she didn't want to get too far away from his protection.

Derek caught up in a couple of long strides and resisted the urge to cup her elbow. "So you're more than halfway through law school and now have a summer internship? Your parents must be proud." His head pounded at the memory of her father, Mr. Willford McClarnon, shoe-manufacturing mogul and commander in chief of the McClarnon family.

She tossed a quizzical glance his way as they entered the elevator. He pushed the button for the third floor. "You never met them, did you? Father has a business reputation to uphold, and Mother has endless garden club meetings. There's no place for a daughter to be a lawyer in their world. If Michael had attended law school, it would have been perfect. He would be the perfect son. But the lines are clearly drawn between what's appropriate for a girl and what's appropriate for a boy. Lines that haven't changed since the 1950s." She inhaled a deep but ragged breath and shook her head slightly as if she'd said too much. "No. They're not proud. They didn't want me to go to law school."

Derek gripped the handrail. He wasn't surprised. Rather, a powerful wave of sympathy rocked through him. "Your father ought to embrace your ambition and bring you on as a corporate lawyer. Surely with a company that large he has need of many lawyers."

"He hires all he needs." The elevator doors opened, and after a quick scan of the elevator well, Derek let Hannah step out first. "The society my parents circulate in is very old-fashioned. Women are expected to volunteer and have hair appointments and gossip over chicken-salad sandwiches for lunch at the country club. Women don't work, let alone in a profession where men wear the suits."

Pausing outside the law offices, he flashed her a wry grin. "So you're the family rebel." He'd known she had some independent tendencies given their history together, but he hadn't figured it would go this far, to buck her parents' expectations.

"My father is part of an old-boys network that works for his business. He's not enough of a rebel to start a new trend. Everyone has to make their choices. This seems to be God's will for me, and I choose His ways."

At least she had parents who cared about her. Derek pulled the door open for her and watched her heels make footprints in the carpet as she strode into the reception area. She hadn't been forced to finish her teen years with an aunt and uncle who thought she was an imposition.

God's will. Had that been God's will for him, his parents' deaths when he was just a young teen? What a struggle of faith that had brought about over the years. And yet, here, right in front of him, was the reason he knew God had blessed him. The very woman who had helped his faith grow into something bigger and better. Despite his struggles, he knew the blessings had been plentiful, first with a position at the Heartwood Hill Police Department, then with a good friend like Reid Palmer, and now with a new position with the FBI with plenty of hope and possibility.

But first, he needed to get through this first assignment with his former love at his side. Those old feelings of inadequacy surfaced from wherever he had squashed them years ago and threatened to choke him. He tamped them down with a hard swallow and followed Hannah into the office. Despite all the time he had spent preparing for this moment, he still had no idea how to break the news. News that, most likely, would rip her world apart.

TWO

Could there be any further surprises today?

Hannah shook out her ruffled turquoise skirt and tugged at the hem of her black cardigan with trembling hands as she turned down the hallway and headed toward her desk. A nervous perspiration stuck to her like humidity on a muggy August day, but there was nothing she could do about it.

Maybe she should apply for a gun permit. Her brother had one, and her father certainly kept firearms in his safe room at their home. But a McClarnon woman with a little pink pistol in her purse? Then again, after heading off to law school, would a concealed-carry permit really be that shocking to her father?

Hannah drew in a shuddery breath, still trying to process the fact that she'd almost been killed today. If it wasn't for Derek Chambers, of all people, who'd jumped into the fray on her behalf, who knew what might have happened. It was a blessing that he'd made an appointment to see her, though she still had no clue why. She never thought she'd see him again, especially considering the way he'd ditched her almost ten years ago.

She sighed, desperately wishing she could dash out for a few minutes alone and collect her thoughts, but the expectation to appear professional and get through whatever it was he needed to tell her weighed on her.

Before she could reach her desk, Mallory stepped out of her office and enveloped her in a warm hug. "Reid told me to stay here but I was desperate to come down and see if you were okay. Are you all right?"

"I'm fine. A little shaky, but unharmed."

"What a relief! No ambulance arrived, so I figured no one was hurt, but I still couldn't help worrying." She glanced behind Hannah.

Hannah turned to include Derek in the conversation. "This is Derek Chambers, FBI. Derek, this is my employer, Mallory Callahan. Apparently, he's our six-o'clock appointment?"

"Yes. The timing of your appointment seems to have been rather fortuitous. I'm glad you were there for her, Derek. Thank you."

Mallory motioned to her office. "Shall we get started?"

"I think I ought to talk to Hannah first, and then we'll proceed from there."

"Fine. Take all the time you need." A quizzical look crossed her boss's face, but then she smiled warmly and returned to her office.

Hannah continued to lead Derek down the hall. She spotted his reflection in the glass of a framed print on the wall, and couldn't help noticing how fine he looked in his khaki cargo pants and his navy button-front shirt, which hid his shoulder holster. He wasn't a thin and gangly teen boy anymore, but a well-muscled and self-possessed man. Still, though, his law-enforcement position wouldn't fit with her parents' high-society world, no matter how much strength and self-command he exuded. They appreciated and supported the work of men in uniform, but guys like him weren't exactly a part of the high-powered board meetings and fancy dinner-party circuit.

The muscles around her smile spasmed as she pointed Derek toward the chair next to her desk. "Have a seat. Will this take long? I have a few things I'd like to get done before I go home tonight." And it probably wasn't best if he stuck around any longer than absolutely necessary anyway. Even with another disappearing act, it would be difficult to tuck the memory of Derek Chambers into the recesses of her mind now.

Without an answer, he graced her with another subtle grin, the dimples in the corners of his mouth slanting into pleasant lines, like he was remembering a good joke or a fond occurrence.

Hannah sighed. What had happened to her day that she had so carefully planned out? Could her heart take much more?

He seemed at a loss for words as he pressed his lips together and looked everywhere but at her. This couldn't be good, although she couldn't fathom what this could be about. Sure, she had her difficulties, but nothing that would warrant the appearance of an FBI agent. "So, you said you're with the Bureau? Is that why you're here?"

"Yes." He cleared his throat and met her gaze. "I actually just graduated from the academy, and have been given my first assignment."

"And what is this first assignment?"

"You. My supervisor thought it best to send an agent you already know and, I hope, trust.

I know it's been a long time since we've seen each other, Hannah, and I realize what I'm about to tell you is going to come as a huge shock. But I need you to believe me and trust me."

She crossed her arms over her middle and waited for him to continue.

"The FBI's organized crime division has an agent on the inside of a crime family out of Chicago, and he discovered that a long time ago, one of their family captains had a baby with his girlfriend. When that little daughter was about a year old, the girlfriend and the baby went missing. Agents found her car. It had gone over a precipice and crashed in the field below. There was blood and hair in the car, but no bodies. She and the daughter had just disappeared, and local law enforcement ran out of leads. Case closed, or so they thought."

"How terrible." A million sympathetic thoughts and questions raced through Hannah's mind, all left unspoken as Derek continued the narrative.

"Apparently, this captain had his suspicions about his family and this mysterious car crash. I don't know what he knew or suspected, but our guy on the inside just recently got intel that he has been looking for them. Now, we have information that he has found the mother."

"She's alive? Is she all right?" What this had to do with her, Hannah had no idea. But it was an interesting story. She uncrossed her arms and leaned on the desk, anxious to hear the rest of the tale.

"She's alive, and we have agents looking for her. Through the mother, we believe, that captain has also found the daughter. As you can imagine, we're not anticipating a happy family reunion. Both of them are in danger." Derek leaned forward in his chair, an intensity lighting his brown eyes, and enveloped her small hands in his. "Hannah, you are the daughter."

"I'm *what*?" Her heart seemed to stop for a moment as she scrambled to process what this would mean. The huge upset it would cause to her world. But it couldn't possibly be true. She was a McClarnon. Wasn't she? She shook her head slowly, keeping her eyes closed to lessen the dizziness that threatened her, and pulled her hands away. "That can't be right. You're thinking of someone else."

"No. You are the daughter." He spoke slowly

as if giving her time to breathe in between each word. "You're adopted."

"And how do you think you know this? I haven't seen you since high school, and now you show up out of the blue to tell me that I'm not the daughter of my parents? How dare you!" She moved to pound a fist on her desk, but Derek grabbed her hand.

"I'm sorry, Hannah." He held her hands in both of his once again as he recounted all the pertinent details of this child's birth—the place, the date, the time.

With each statement, Hannah wanted to tell Derek it wasn't possible, that the little girl couldn't have possibly been her. But her throat had choked each time, like trying to swallow a pill that was too big for her. "So, Mother and Father are..." If all this was true, what were they?

"They're still your mother and father. Your relationship with them hasn't changed and doesn't need to change. But now you know they are your adoptive parents. Your mother didn't give birth to you." He looked around the cubical as if trying to give her a little space. "So you had no idea you were adopted?"

"No, assuming that what you're telling me

is even true, which I doubt. They've just always been my parents. Why would I think anything else?" She paused as his words sank into her consciousness. Her mind could barely absorb it all. Didn't *want* to absorb it all. "You said the mother and daughter were in danger. So, that's why that guy shot at me? He knew who I was even before you told me what you know? I thought I knew who I was, but now I'm not so sure."

"You are still the same person, Hannah. But yes, he was here for you. That's why I'm here. To protect you. I just didn't think they'd find you so fast."

"So, was that the man who you say is my birth father? Do you think he'll be back?" She fluttered her hands to her neck, but it didn't soothe her like she had hoped.

"No, most likely it was not your birth father. He may be in the area nearby, but he would have sent one of his men. And yes, that man will be back."

"What else do you know? I need to know everything."

"There's not much more, I'm afraid. We've never had enough evidence to arrest him, so our knowledge is limited. I've just been brought on the case recently because of my—" he cleared his throat "—friendship with you. My supervising agent believes that your birth father thinks you may know something or have something that would incriminate him. For that reason alone, he would be willing to eliminate you."

Hannah's stomach flip-flopped at the word *eliminate*. "As we have already established, I didn't even know I was adopted. That is, if it's even true. How could I possibly incriminate him? I have several favorite things from when I was a child, but they all came from my parents." She took a mental inventory of her old belongings. Her father had encouraged her to clean out some things from her childhood, but she couldn't bear to part with them. *Sentimental*, he'd called her. *A pack rat*. But she hadn't seen the harm in keeping a few boxes of mementos in the back of the closet. "I honestly can't think of anything."

"Perhaps there's nothing, but my mission right now is to keep you safe."

"So far, you've done a fine job." Hannah forced a smile. She might not trust Derek any longer with her heart, but she would trust him with her life. "I think I better talk to Mallory and fill her in."

"I'll wait outside the door if you'd like some privacy."

She stood and Derek followed suit. "For now, yes, I'd appreciate that."

As she made her way toward Mallory's office, Hannah shot a glance back at Derek and mouthed *thank you*, then whispered a prayer for calmness and wisdom as she knocked on her boss's door. Surely, she was safe here in the building. The shooter had left. But it was still a comfort to know that the broad-shouldered, strapping FBI agent would be nearby with his trusty weapon at the ready. Just in case.

At Mallory's call to come in, Hannah opened the door and stepped inside. Her boss sat behind her desk and pointed Hannah toward a floral upholstered chair. She clutched her skirt in her fists and teetered on the edge of the chair. "Do you have a few minutes?" She licked her dry lips.

"Of course." Mallory came around the desk and sat in the other client chair, waiting for Hannah to continue.

Hannah pushed herself back into the upholstery. She wasn't really sure what she was asking for, if anything. After all, she'd only been working there a few weeks, and now she was apparently causing a threatening situation to the office. Mallory didn't seem upset about it, but could this cost her the summer job? Who would want an intern who brought danger to the premises?

After law school, it would be back to her parents' mansion and the life of a spinster, pro bono attorney. At least she could practice law, after a fashion. She and her father had reached a truce, and she was determined to keep her end of it for the sake of her family. But for now, this was her freedom. "I'm not quite sure how to approach this, but you need to know. Derek is here to protect me. It seems the FBI is investigating a crime family with which they think I have some connection."

Mallory's eyebrows lifted slightly, but otherwise she maintained a neutral lawyer's expression.

Hannah clutched her skirt more tightly. "It turns out that I'm adopted. At least, that's what they say. Derek says my birth father is with the Mafia, and he's looking for me." She let out a long breath, which she'd been holding, seemingly since Derek had broken the news.

"Wow. That's some big news." Mallory

leaned forward and laid a hand on Hannah's forearm. "Why does the FBI believe you're adopted?"

"Details of my birth. Adoption records. Derek's just recently become involved." She raced through a dozen different memories from her childhood, but no clue emerged about her adoption. "I have my birth certificate, and Father and Mother are listed as my parents, but I can't say I've ever read it thoroughly."

"Your birth certificate wouldn't show that you were adopted, except for the discrepancy in the dates. Your parents would have a court-issued decree that finalized the adoption."

Hannah furrowed her brow. "What do you mean by a discrepancy in the dates?"

"The firm has copies of your birth certificate and your driver's license in your personnel folder from when you began employment here. I can pull it up if you'd like." Mallory returned to her desk and her computer. Soon, a printer on her credenza was spitting out a copy of Hannah's birth certificate, which her boss handed over.

Hannah stared at the dates but had no idea what she was looking for. Her heart thumped, but she didn't move so she wouldn't betray her anxiety. "What should I see here?"

Mallory leaned over the desk. "Your birth certificate has definitely been amended. See? Here is your birth date." She moved her finger down the paper. "And here is the issue date. It's over a year later. There's no reason for it to be any more than a month or two after the fact unless the time was needed to finalize an adoption."

The pounding of Hannah's heart moved to her head until the edge of the room turned fuzzy. "So, it could be true. My birth certificate proves it." Tacky sweat inched through her blouse and the fuzziness stood at the edge of her vision, threatening to consume her.

"Whatever is going on, it'll be fine. Trust in the Lord to reveal whatever you need to know when you need to know it. And from the looks of it you have a valiant protector in Derek." Mallory's lowered tone fought through the haze. "It doesn't change who your parents are or who you are."

Hannah gulped in breaths that didn't seem to reach her lungs. The fuzziness marched in on her like a swarm of grasshoppers. Through the haze, she saw Mallory come back around the desk and sit in the other client chair. Her warm hand covered Hannah's, her smooth, reassuring touch a rhythmic call back to the present.

"I need to talk to my mother." She forced a strong tone, one she didn't feel but desperately needed to push away the dark cloud that threatened to envelop her. "And my father." Oh, her father. What would he have to say about this?

"Yes. Talk to them. And at some point, you may want to search for your birth mother." Compassion flooded Mallory's voice, and Hannah appreciated her delicacy. "But I want to warn you. If you do search, you may not be happy with what you find. Or you may not find anything at all. We don't know how much the FBI knows about her past, her circumstances or even her location."

The surrealistic nature of those options settled on her shoulders like a heavy cloak, and Hannah couldn't force out an answer.

Mallory patted her hand. "Talking to your parents is a good place to start. But whatever news they may have, if any at all—" she paused for emphasis "—try to stay calm. Now, I will help you in any way I can if this turns out to be true. I'm willing to talk anytime, and now you have my personal phone number." She scribbled on the back of a business card and pressed it into Hannah's hand. "Go now, if you feel you need to, and the job is here whenever. A lot has happened, so take whatever time you need."

After flashing her boss a grateful look, Hannah focused on the seven digits on the card until she could stand steady. "What a day." Her stomach flip-flopped. Her parents had some explaining to do. She knew what her next move was—to get some answers and, hopefully, to stay safe.

"Are you two all right?"

Derek accepted the firm handshake of his old pal Reid Palmer. "We're fine. Thanks for your help down there."

"No problem. You've got a lot going on."

"Yes, but not as much as Hannah. She just found out she's adopted, her birth father is a Mafia boss and I'm the one who had to tell her." He crossed his arms over his chest and touched his fingers to the thumb break on his shoulder holster. "Hannah's really shaken up, understandably so. But she's resilient. Tougher than she used to be. She's going to need to be, with the danger she's in."

From his vantage point down the hallway,

Derek saw the door to Mallory's office swing open. But no one emerged.

He hadn't let down his guard since the attack less than an hour ago, despite the fact that he saw the shooter speed away. But surely they were safe up here. There were only two doors to the suite of offices. The back door was locked, and Derek and Reid stood within view of the front door. No one had come or gone.

He moved to the window at the end of the hallway that overlooked the parking lot. The truck had not returned. But the office only faced out one side of the building, so he had no way to check all entrances and side streets. Wherever Hannah thought she was going next, Derek would not leave her side.

Voices filtered down the hallway, but he couldn't make out any words. He nodded toward the open door. "What do you make of that?"

Reid shrugged. "They're almost done." Apparently, his friend wasn't on alert, despite his own little difficulty a year or so ago with his wife, Samantha. At the time she had been on the run from a thug who had tried to kidnap her adopted daughter, Lily, and had crashed into Reid's car. The end result was a harrowing two days and eventually their wedding. "Congrats on your graduation from the FBI academy, by the way. You were one of the best officers on the Heartwood Hill PD to work with, but sometimes we move on to other things. This your first assignment?"

"Yes. Quite a start, don't you think?"

Reid raised his eyebrows. "Is there a history here? With Hannah?"

"Yes." Derek jammed his hands in his pockets. "That's why I'm here. My supervising agent thought it best if the FBI sent someone Hannah knows. What they don't know are the details of our past."

"And?"

"We dated secretly in high school our senior year. Her family is super wealthy and upper class. My aunt and uncle were most definitely not upper class. We knew her parents would never approve, so we kept it a secret. Nearly every Friday night, we would go to the library to study. She just didn't tell her parents that she was with me. We would drive in to the Indianapolis library, where no one knew us except the librarians, and they didn't care." Images of a seventeen-year-old Hannah contrasted in his thoughts with the

Hannah he had rescued today. She had only grown more beautiful. More compelling.

"Let me guess." A frown creased Reid's brow. "Someone found out."

Derek nodded. "Her father." He shrugged, but tension made it difficult to relax his shoulders again. "I don't know how. I just know that one day we were planning on attending college together, and the next, I was summoned to the McClarnons'. Her father told me clearly that I was to leave her alone. What else could I do? Mr. McClarnon was—is—a powerful man. I didn't want to get on his wrong side. I knew I wasn't good enough for her anyway. We had been naive to think that a relationship could work."

"So you didn't see her again?"

"I saw her at graduation a couple of days later. I never got close enough to talk to her. That was it. She went away to college. Her parents moved from Heartwood Hill to Lafayette, an hour away. The end."

"Are you sure?"

"Yes." She wasn't his Hannah any longer. Never would be.

"Does she know her father forbade you from seeing her?"

That was the toughest part. "No." Mr.

McClarnon had also strongly suggested that Derek not tell Hannah anything of their meeting. As far as she knew, he had just abandoned the relationship.

Derek prayed for the strength and tenacity to complete this first assignment for the FBI. He was over her, right? The fact that there had been no one else in the intervening years simply attested to his devotion to his job. But he couldn't help wondering if his superior had known the specifics of their romantic past, would he have assigned someone else?

It didn't matter now. He was here, standing in the hallway waiting for the beautiful and sweet Hannah McClarnon to emerge from a meeting with her employer. This mission had no close alignment with his heart. It was just the first in what would hopefully be a long line of successful missions in his future.

Reid shifted to lean against a doorjamb, pulling Derek's focus from his inner thoughts, and nodded toward the office where Hannah was. "So what about her birth family?"

"I don't know a lot." He jammed his fists in his pockets as if that could release some of his pent-up frustration. "The short version is that we have an informant on the inside of a crime family operating out of Chicago.

One of their so-called captains has been looking for a former girlfriend and their daughter that disappeared over twenty years ago. Now, he's found the girlfriend. We believe that the girlfriend was forced to give up information about the daughter. That daughter is Hannah."

"And the birth mother?"

"I don't know. That's not part of my mission, but I do know the FBI hasn't located her yet."

"I don't know how much help I could be, but if there's anything, don't hesitate." Reid clapped him on the shoulder. "Even though we're not on the force together any longer, we're a part of a brotherhood. And after the way you saved my bacon last year, you know I'll do whatever I can to help you out."

"Thanks." Derek appreciated the vote of confidence. He nodded toward the voices coming from the office. "You have any read on her?"

"Hannah? She hasn't been here long. Just started a few weeks ago, and she works primarily with Mallory. But I've heard both Mallory and Samantha say that she's smart and reliable, both excellent qualities for a future lawyer."

"Yes, she was the same in high school."

Hannah stepped out of the office, followed by Mallory. Hannah's stunning beauty made Derek's mouth feel like sandpaper, and he swallowed hurriedly to cover the effect she had on him. He couldn't let that get in the way of his mission. Get it done and move on. That was his mantra.

But he couldn't look away. She still seemed stricken. Upset. Whatever had been said in that meeting didn't appear to have lessened the sting of receiving life-altering news that had rocked her to the core. He wanted to go to her, fold her in his arms, stroke her silky hair and whisper to her that all would be well. But not only did he not know if that was true, especially considering what she had just learned that afternoon, but it also wouldn't do either of their hearts any good to follow the inclinations that would undoubtedly only lead to more crushing despair.

He clenched his fists in his pockets, working valiantly to shift his gaze to the floor, to the window, to anywhere but at her. Reid's lowered voice sounded near his ear. "She does have a certain quiet beauty, but that's all I'll say. I'm a happily married man, late for supper with my wife and daughter."

Derek shook his hand and watched his

buddy leave through the back door. He stared at the closed door for a few moments, forcing his thoughts back to the assignment. It was time to move on.

Hannah thanked Mallory and then motioned Derek into the tiny break room. "Would you like a cup of coffee? I can't imagine I need the caffeine after the news you just dropped on me. But maybe holding the warm mug would help?" She turned to grab the canister of coffee and kept her back turned slightly to Derek, but he could still see that she fumbled for a paper towel from the roll on the counter and then dabbed her eyes.

He cleared his throat gently. "Sure, coffee sounds good. Why don't you sit down and I'll get it?"

She sniffled and pushed the paper towel in her pocket before she turned to him. A tentative smile flickered on her lips. "If you don't mind, I'd appreciate it."

"Of course."

From what he had seen out of the hallway window, it seemed that there was no sign of the truck or even any vehicle that seemed suspicious. The red-and-blue flashing lights of law enforcement were still visible in the parking lot below. Derek relaxed a bit but kept his attention trained on the door. Hannah could have a little bit more time to process this new information, but at some point, they would have to move on.

As her sniffling subsided behind him, he started the coffeemaker and retrieved a couple of mugs from the cabinet. A few minutes later, he settled into the chair across from her and poured a touch of creamer in his mug.

Hannah added sugar and creamer, then sipped gingerly from the cup. She had regained some composure, perhaps from holding her polka-dotted mug as if it was a life preserver, appearing as if some of the upset was being replaced with something else. Frustration, maybe?

"How was your meeting with Mallory?" Derek leaned forward on the table. It wouldn't be difficult to create a sense of intimacy in such a tiny space, an intimacy that he hoped would make Hannah more comfortable. "I know we haven't seen each other in a few years, but you can still talk to me."

She sipped again. "You always were a good listener. I liked that about you." A tentative smile wobbled across her face.

"I liked listening to you."

"Mallory confirmed that I was probably

adopted, like you said. It's just so hard to believe, so she pulled my birth certificate from my personnel file. She pointed out that the date of my birth and the issue date of the certificate were a year apart, a discrepancy that only happens when a birth certificate is amended by an adoption finalization." A tear leaked down her cheek, and she retrieved the paper towel from her pocket to dab it away.

He blew out a breath he hadn't realized he had been holding. "Okay."

"I'm in my twenties, and my parents never told me? And what about Michael, my brother? Is he adopted?"

Derek just shrugged. It was probably best he not say anything but give her time and space to talk.

"You know Michael. You two hung out in high school." Hannah paused, her face screwed up in an expression of contemplation. "He so obviously looks like Father that I doubt he's adopted as well. But did he know all these years that I was adopted?"

"Does it matter?" He turned his mug around, studying all the sides. "It sounds like you don't know for sure, so let's not jump to any conclusions."

"You're right. I don't know." She flipped

her dark hair behind her shoulder and stood. "I need to go talk to my parents. Immediately. They need to tell me the truth."

"Now?" He mentally ran through a few scenarios. Going to Hannah's parents' house was actually a good idea. Houses like the McClarnon mansion always had top-of-the-line security in place, as well as a household staff. And he was definitely in favor of vacating the last place the shooter had seen them both— right here, outside this law office in downtown Heartwood Hill.

"Yes. Now. It's Monday evening, so they'll be at home." She checked her watch. "Right about now, Mother will be supervising the washing of the supper dishes before the maid goes home, and Father will be reading a classic novel, something like Dickens or Hugo or Tolstoy. He meticulously sets aside a half hour each night to read and refuses to be interrupted. Lafayette is less than an hour away, so I can make it before it gets too late." She had one foot pointed toward the door. "I'll just grab my bag."

"Are they really that predictable?"

"For years now. They have a schedule, and they stick to it." Hannah lowered her voice to a man's husky pitch. "'That's how you get ahead.' That's what my father always says."

He couldn't let her go by herself, not with that attack earlier. His assignment was to protect her at all costs and that's exactly what he'd be doing. "I'll drive you. That doesn't sound like a conversation you should have alone." At her startled look, he continued. "I won't say anything, but at least you'll have someone by your side and a listening ear when all is done. And I can keep you safe as we travel. Just in case."

Her expression softened, the fine lines around her eyes crinkling with appreciation. "I guess you are my law-enforcement hero. Between the shooter and then the information about being adopted, I'm a little shaken." She held up her small, delicate hands. "Okay, a lot shaken. Overwhelmed, really. I could use the company."

Hannah retrieved her purse, and they rode the elevator down to the first floor. With the parking lot clear of present danger, Derek ushered Hannah back to his Ford Escape.

This was a turn of events he had anticipated, but that didn't ease the nervous wrenching in his gut now that the moment had arrived. He was to come face-to-face with Hannah's father again, after the first, and only time, they had ever spoken. Without a doubt, he still wasn't good enough for their polite society, despite the badge and title he now proudly carried.

Lord, give me strength and wisdom with the McClarnons.

He never thought he would see them again, and now he was bringing their daughter back with a potentially deadly situation in tow.

THREE

As they sped down Interstate 65 toward her parents' home, Hannah prayed for strength and wisdom and comfort. Being a victim of violence was unheard of in her circles. Her father kept weapons in the house, but she'd never really been around them. And learning that she was adopted had upset her more than she wanted to admit. She loved her parents more than anyone on the face of the planet and wanted to please them, but now that she knew she was adopted, then what? Who was she? And who were her parents?

She tugged her purse off the floor of Derek's SUV and dug around for the mints she always carried. The corner of a package scraped her hand. She grasped it and pulled out the box that had arrived in her mailbox earlier that day. Without time then, she had grabbed the package from the mail on her way to the interview and stashed it in her bag to open later. Centered on her lap, she studied the computer-generated return-address label that said it was from "Dad." That was a little odd since he had always been "Father." Hannah couldn't recall a time she had ever called him by that casual moniker.

She placed her bag back on the floor and wiggled a finger under the corner of the wrapping. Maybe this was some kind of affirmation from him, some acceptance of her desire for a career in law. It was doubtful, but a girl could hope.

Derek ceased his scanning of the road around them long enough to glance at the package. His eyebrows lifted into question marks, but he remained silent. Hannah appreciated that he wouldn't pry, but there was no harm in telling him. He had never met her father, and her father knew nothing of their secret romance in high school, so perhaps it would help him if he knew a bit of the man going in.

"I received this today from my father, and this is the first chance I've had to open it." She tore away the paper and revealed a small box with a hinged lid. Inside, nestled in the white fabric lining, sat a wristwatch with a black leather strap and a brass case. The face was creamy white with the scales of justice engraved on it. "It's beautiful."

She held it out to Derek, and he glanced at it. "Nice. That was thoughtful of him."

Hannah pulled it back and studied it. "Maybe he's finally beginning to see that this is God's path for me. Law school."

"They don't approve? Are you there against their will?"

Good question. Was she going against their will? She and her father had had their disagreement about school, but he had acquiesced. Of course, a job after graduation was another hurdle to jump. "I don't think I'd say I'm defying them… I wouldn't risk that. But they expect me to marry someone within their circles and then live a life of charity events and country-club dances and garden-club meetings. What they refuse to see is that I don't want a life like that for myself. I would be so bored. So unfulfilled. I want to do more."

"Do you doubt their faith?" he asked.

"No. I doubt their acknowledgment that I'm a grown-up with faith of my own, and that I'm also able to discern God's will, especially for my life."

"Well said, counselor." He tossed a smile in her direction.

She strapped the watch on her wrist and held her arm out, admiring the sparkle of the brass case and ignoring what his dimpled grin did to her insides. "While we're there, I'll thank him for it, but he may not even know exactly what he sent. He probably had an assistant choose it and mail it."

"Still, though, it was a thoughtful gesture."

He was right, of course. Hannah stared out the window as they rode the next several miles in silence. Freshly plowed and planted fields shone in the evening sun, and Hannah inhaled deeply of Derek's scent, a mingling of fresh laundry detergent and spicy aftershave. It was aromatherapy, a healing oil that brought peace and calm.

That calm disappeared when Derek spoke again, a huskiness creeping into his voice. "So are we going to talk about us? About this awkwardness?"

Oh, no. "No. I'd rather keep the awkwardness than dredge up the past. It doesn't matter anyway right now, does it?" He'd left once. She wasn't going to let him get close enough to hurt her again.

"It wasn't what you thought."

How could he possibly know what she thought? And why did he have to bring it up now? Did he really think she needed this, too, today? "It's fine, Derek. Whatever. It's in the past."

"I just think you should know…"

A vehicle in her side mirror grabbed her attention and jolted her heart until she clutched at her shoulder belt as it looped across her chest. Was that the same truck as before?

She stared into the mirror, the sound of Derek's voice drowned out by the drumming of her pulse.

"Hannah? What is it?"

She spun to look out the back window, crouching low behind the headrest. "I think that's the same truck that followed me earlier, on the way to the interview. Is that a badge-shaped decal in the front window?"

"Yes. It's been following us for a couple of miles now. I think we need to lose it."

"We're almost to Lafayette." She turned back to face front, clutching and twisting the hem of her shirt. "Are we going to lead him right to Father and Mother?"

"Not if I can help it." Still peering into the rearview mirror, Derek grabbed the steering wheel with both hands. "Hold on."

Hannah grasped the door handle with her right hand and the edge of the seat with her left as he pulled hard on the wheel. The little SUV cut across two lanes of traffic and veered down the exit ramp toward South Street. A whiff of exhaust and warm rubber assaulted her as she fought to stay upright in her seat. Multiple car horns protested the rudeness of the truck's driver as a blur of black followed them down the ramp.

"He's still tailing us. Now what?" Her palm slicked against the handle. She dried it on her skirt and prayed silently for safety and security.

"We keep going." Derek was so focused on the road that he didn't even glance at her. "Remember, we're in the lead, deciding where to go. He has to react. That gives us the advantage."

At the bottom of the ramp, he turned west. The evening sun was just above the horizon, blinding in its intensity. Hannah slapped down the visor, but it didn't reach low enough. The truck squealed through a yellow light to follow them.

"How can you see? Shouldn't we turn out of the sun? An accident won't help us now."

"Affirmative. Hold on." At the next thoroughfare, he made a fast and hard right. Hannah barely had a chance to glance at the street sign. Sagamore Parkway. The name seemed familiar, but the surroundings did not. Her parents had moved to Lafayette after she had graduated high school, so although it had been her legal domicile through college and law school, she wasn't familiar enough with the city to know where they were. Truth be told, she had barely wandered any farther from her parents' mansion than to the local branch of the library and the mall.

The black truck followed, but Hannah noted with satisfaction that two cars separated them and more traffic traveled just ahead of them. She couldn't quite see the face of the driver, to make visual confirmation that it was the same man as before, especially in the gathering gloom of evening and with that distance between them. But the truck was the same, so the driver was mostly likely the same as well.

Derek screeched the SUV left, again into the sun, on Union Street.

A shiver threatened as Hannah read the road signs. "We're in a school zone." She pointed to the left, and he swiveled for a quick glance. "Multiple school zones. We can't do that slow speed. What is it, twenty miles per hour? Look at all those buildings. He'll catch up for sure."

"It's late. School's out." He released a hand from his grip on the wheel long enough to squeeze her hand as it clutched the seat. "No need to slow down."

His hand radiated warmth and gave her a sense of security, but a glance in the side mirror revealed the truck still barreling down on them. "So now what? Could you take him?"

"I'd rather not find out. Not by myself." Derek jerked the steering wheel, turning them south onto North 18th Street. Houses flew by on the right, and the school zone ended at what the sign said was Murdock Park. It looked like it could be a good place to hide, but there were no roads.

"So where do we go? Drive on the sidewalk?" She pointed to the park and the wide walking path that entered into a wooded area.

The truck blared its horn and crossed into oncoming traffic to blow past a blue sedan. It was now only one car behind. Derek glanced in the mirror again and gritted his teeth. "No. This isn't an action movie. That wouldn't be safe for pedestrians, and it would draw too much attention to us." He pulled the car onto a small residential road. "Here."

"So we keep turning until he can't catch up? Like how when a crocodile attacks, you're supposed to run in a zigzag pattern because they can't turn that well?" Law was supposed to be safe. Free from physical harm. She hadn't joined the police force or the CIA. There had been no training in law school for outrunning bad guys.

"That's a myth. Not true."

"What? That's not what we're doing?"

"Not true about crocodiles. For us, yes. We're eluding capture."

The SUV bumped through an intersection and exited the residential area for a commercial zone. Instead of houses, there were passing businesses and strip malls, with only two or three separate shops dotting the sides of the street.

"We'll be fine. I see something up ahead. Hopefully, this is the last time I'll have to tell you to hold on."

Hannah dug her feet into the floorboard as Derek bounced the vehicle over the curb and into the parking lot of a funeral home. Great. Well, at least they were in the right place if the shooter did catch up to them. She shot up a prayer as they turned around back. *Lord, I love You, but I'm not ready to meet my maker.*

He tore through the parking lot and around the side of the two-story brick structure that looked like it used to be a fine, older home. A detached garage with an open bay door beckoned around the back. Derek pulled the Escape into the space that was large enough for a hearse and jumped out. Hannah followed but crouched down at his command to stay low, as he raced to the side door and then punched a button on the wall.

The garage door began to close.

Derek signaled to her, and she crept toward the hood of the car, deeper into the garage, until she met him at the hood. He put an arm around her shoulders, a help to keep her steady and a strength to comfort her as they watched the door close. They were soon swallowed in complete darkness.

She held her breath, the perspiration trickling down her back marching side by side with a tingle of apprehension, as they waited for the truck to come roaring through the parking lot and crash through the door. But all she could hear was her heart beating.

"Is that it? Are we safe?" She kept her

whisper so soft she could barely discern her own voice.

"I think so." Derek's hoarse whisper tickled her ear, and another tingle traversed her spine, this one for different reasons but still full of apprehension. "Let me grab my phone."

The glow of the screen illuminated his face and the grim set of his mouth. With the tap of an icon, the phone's flashlight illuminated their part of the garage.

"Are they gone?" Derek lowered his arm, and a chill immediately set in to Hannah's shoulders. "How did they find us?"

"I don't know yet, but I think you need to call your parents and let them know we're coming. If you go see them in person, they might want to make sure their security is in order."

"What? No. I need to spring it on them in person. See their reactions for myself. That'll get to the truth of the matter. And not to worry, their security is always top-notch. Besides, that truck is gone. We lost him."

He laid a hand on her arm, but this time it felt restrictive. "I still think you should call."

She shoved herself up to her feet. "It's not up to you." An angry tone entered, and she stopped herself. She didn't want to be that person. With a deep breath, she tried again, this time more level. "I will drive myself to my parents' house if I need to, leaving you here at the funeral home." She gestured around the darkness. "Rather, in the garage."

Maneuvering in the dim light of his phone flashlight, she tiptoed around him and toward the driver's door. "Hannah." His tone was warm and wrapped around her like a thick quilt.

A quaver crawled up her throat, and she swallowed hard to tamp it down. "I'm sorry. It's just so much to process. You've never found out anything like this—that you're adopted."

"No." He stepped closer. "You remember. I was raised by my aunt and uncle after my parents were killed. But I'd like to think I have a little idea of what you're feeling. Confusion. Betrayal. Curiosity."

"Oh, Derek. I do remember. I wasn't thinking." She had known he was living with an aunt and uncle, and he had mentioned, all those years ago, that his mom and dad had passed away. But she didn't know any more than that. There was clearly more to Derek Chambers than she had realized. She placed a hand on his arm, a zing in the darkness striking to her core. "I'm sorry. We didn't talk about it much."

She sensed, more than saw, his shrug. "It didn't seem important at the time. I wanted to think about us and our future, not my past."

"Then you really do know what I'm feeling. You understand the importance of getting the truth."

"Yes. I do." A steely determination had crept into his tone.

She stepped again toward the driver-side door. "So, who's driving?"

Derek glanced at the sign that read Union Street as he turned back onto the side street that seemed to widen out in the next block or so. He'd settled Hannah into the passenger seat, and now he was following her directions as she got her bearings in a town she didn't know all that well.

The scent of gasoline and death lingered in his nostrils from the funeral home's garage. Maybe it was just his imagination, the idea of the scent of death. Maybe it was a memory from witnessing the murder of his parents. But even if it was, he still wiggled his nose in an attempt to eradicate the aroma before he could be inundated with images he had struggled to forget.

His cell phone vibrated next to his hip, and he grabbed it from the holster on his belt. A square popped up on his incoming-call screen. His supervising agent's code name for himself. So newly graduated from the academy that the protective plastic coating was barely pulled off his badge, Derek knew he'd have to check in frequently.

He glanced at Hannah, relieved that she didn't seem to be paying attention to his phone. Being around her again made him jittery, and he didn't want to mess up in front of his supervising agent. "Go."

Square's voice was hoarse in his ear. "Secure?"

"For now."

"Did you acquire the subject?"

The subject seemed a harsh way of communicating about the complex yet feminine woman who sat beside him. "Yes."

"Is there knowledge?" Square was asking if Derek had informed Hannah of her adoption and the identity of her birth father.

"Affirmative."

Hannah looked over at him, a question in her wide, brown eyes. Derek shrugged but didn't respond, an attempt to convey nonchalance. Hopefully, it would calm both of them.

"Location?" The supervising agent would check in regularly with Derek for his first two years as an official FBI agent. But since Derek had just arrived in Heartwood Hill that afternoon, it seemed a little soon for an update. Perhaps that was because the supervisor had been unable to accompany him. Whatever he had to do to comply, though, Derek was willing. He was living his dream, and nothing would stand in his way, not even the beautiful creature who sat in the vehicle with him.

"Sliding into home base." It was summertime, and that meant baseball. Square would understand that Derek had Hannah in transit to her parents' house.

"Okay. Play ball." His supervisor ended the call, and Derek understood that he was to proceed but with extreme caution.

Hannah flipped her brown waves over her shoulder. "Everything okay?"

Derek ran through what she must have heard from his end of the call. It wouldn't have been anything out of the ordinary. "Yeah. Just checking in." She understood the danger, of that he was sure. No need to dwell on it.

As he continued to follow Hannah's directions, the drive wound them through small starter homes to an area of ethnic grocery stores and soccer fields to an upscale mall and eventually to a section of town where Derek guessed the houses were a million dollars or more.

"How long has it been since you've been home?" Despite the gloom of the evening, Derek still saw luxurious, large yards with winding drives, profusions of flowers and statues of footmen holding lanterns at the end of driveways.

"Probably too long, but law school has kept me busy." She pointed to the right. "Turn here."

"What do your parents know? About us? Did you ever tell them anything?" Derek had had his own private conversation with Mr. McClarnon, but Hannah's father had strictly instructed him not to breathe a word to Hannah. For years, he had carried the torment inside of him and now he was to walk right into the presence of the man who had ended it all. And his own daughter didn't know.

Hannah tossed a startled look at him that

quickly morphed into a soft haze, as if she was remembering the good times they had shared. "No. Nothing."

"That was probably wise. What would be the point?" He took in her rich brown hair, her coordinated black-and-turquoise sweater outfit, her designer bag. He didn't know the brand names, and maybe that was the point. He was quickly realizing that he would do anything to protect Hannah, but that also brought the pain of the knowledge that there was zero chance for a relationship. She was beautiful and smart and caring and seemed perfect for him. But he had a career now, the one he had dreamed of since the time his parents were murdered.

How could he ask her to leave her family for him when they had so much to offer and so many resources to provide for her? What kind of jerk would he be if he expected her to give up the love of her parents and brother and sit in a tiny apartment alone, while he went out on mission after mission after mission? He exhaled roughly. Besides, when it came down to it, he wasn't good enough for her anyway.

Derek pulled into the long cement lane that led to the McClarnon mansion. A gar-

dener was pushing a wheelbarrow toward
the back, probably to the garages and out-
buildings, ready to go home for the night. The
house loomed larger than life, gables peaked
into the clouds and three separate chimneys
pierced the night sky. Large beveled windows
reflected his SUV's headlights as he pulled
up next to a wide set of stone steps flanked
on either side by ornate, carved handrails.

Broken cement steps had marked his childhood, steps that had led to a run-down house
owned by his aunt and uncle. They had, he
supposed, graciously allowed him a bedroom
that was probably less than half the size of
Mr. McClarnon's dressing room. Certainly,
finding out she was adopted was a shock to
Hannah, but at least she had parents who
truly loved her and provided for her exceed-
ingly well. His aunt and uncle had made it
abundantly clear that he was a burden, just as
Mr. McClarnon had not minced words when
he had told Derek he was not worthy of Hannah's attention.

Derek swiped a hand over his forehead.
Tiny beads of perspiration had popped up
at the prospect of meeting Mr. McClarnon
again. Truly, he'd rather go toe-to-toe with a

bank robber than that man. But facing him was unavoidable.

Hannah was out of her side of the Escape before Derek could emerge and come around. Just as they reached the front door, it opened. A man held it wide for them. He was dressed as formally as Derek would have been for the high school prom, if he had ever gone, in a black tie over a starched white dress shirt. A gray vest was buttoned from top to bottom under a black morning coat, and a thin stripe ran down his gray trousers. If memory served, this was the same butler who had ushered him into Mr. McClarnon's presence nearly a decade ago.

"Good evening, Miss Hannah. Welcome home."

"Hello, Carson. I assume Mother and Father are in their usual occupations for a Monday evening?"

A sideways glance from the butler crawled over Derek, but he forced himself to stand tall. What kind of FBI agent would he be if he allowed himself to be intimidated?

"Are they not expecting you?"

"Not exactly, but it's urgent." She swept past Carson, who stepped back quickly to allow her space. Derek followed, stretching out to the full inch he had over the man. As they hurried down the well-appointed hallway toward the sitting room, he fought to maintain that height. He would need it in the coming moments.

As they walked, he surveyed the area. Despite what little he knew about the home and what was normal for the McClarnons, it didn't seem that anything was out of order, or that the shooter or his cohorts, whoever they may be, had been around. Still, he knew better than to let his guard down and would continually monitor their surroundings for any potential threat of danger.

Hannah sauntered into the sitting room ahead of him by a few steps, and Derek sniffed the floral perfume of Hannah's mother and heard her surprised greeting before he made his presence known. When Derek entered, Mr. McClarnon pulled back from a one-armed hug with his daughter, spied him and stiffened, the ice in his crystal glass clinking against the side.

"Evelyn." He spoke softly to his wife, and she immediately turned from her happy reunion with her daughter.

Mrs. McClarnon ran a hand down her silk skirt and stepped forward, her face masked with the high-society politeness and artificial hospitality of welcoming someone who was beneath their station. She held out her hand. "Derek, isn't it? Good evening."

"Ma'am." Derek crimped her hand, suppressing a grin at the mischievous thought of whether or not he should kiss it.

Hannah's father cleared his throat, a call to attention. "Well, Mr. Chambers."

"You remember my name." A curious look from Hannah skittered around his peripheral vision, but he didn't make eye contact. He would have some questions to answer, but not yet.

The squeeze on Derek's hand was tight. A challenge. Derek squeezed back, enough to communicate that he wouldn't be intimidated but not enough to hurt the older gentleman.

Mr. McClarnon's eyes burned into Derek's. "Wish I could say it's good to see you again, but here you are with my daughter."

FOUR

How did her father know Derek's name? Willford McClarnon was an astute business-man—aggressive and perhaps even harsh when the occasion called for it. But Hannah also knew him to be polite and hospitable and loving. He had never even met Derek and, in fact, wouldn't have known him at all since their high school romance had been a secret. Still was a secret. Wasn't it?

Hannah shifted from one foot to the other, now uncertain as to what should come next. Would life have been different if they had told her parents? Would they have accepted Derek? Perhaps they should have tried. But one glance at her father, now glaring at Derek and seemingly holding his hand in a death grip, confirmed that their high school deci-sion had been the right one. That old romance was better kept a secret, just as the renewal of her attraction to him should also be kept under wraps. Again and again the thought bounced around her mind: better to get this situation resolved and let Derek go back to wherever he came from.

Her father finally released Derek's hand and turned toward her mother, placing a protective arm around her. They exchanged a glance, but Hannah couldn't read their expressions.

"It's always nice to have a visit from our little girl, even a surprise one." Her father's tone held the hidden meaning that she should have called first, arranged a time, allowed them to prepare tea or some sort of refreshment, perhaps on the veranda.

"I'm not sure how nice you'll think this is, Father." Hannah couldn't believe the words coming out of her mouth. She wasn't being disrespectful, but assertiveness had never been her forte. Perhaps law school had had a positive effect on her confidence. Either that or the news from just an hour ago was enough to embolden her. She pulled her birth certificate from her purse and thrust it toward him. "I have a few questions."

Her father examined the document for a

few seconds, then looked at her with a question of his own in his eyes. "Yes?"

"Derek, a, um, friend from high school who is now in law enforcement, came to the office today and told me that I'm adopted. *Adopted*, Father! And then the lawyer I work for pulled up my birth certificate and said that the date of issue confirms it." She pointed at the birth certificate. "Is that what this means?"

It would have been nearly imperceptible if Hannah hadn't been watching closely, but her father actually slumped his shoulders. Her mother peered over his arm at the birth certificate, then a single tear slowly coursed down her cheek.

For the first time in her memory, her parents were speechless.

The mahogany mantel clock ticked in the silence, and her mother's floral eau de toilette scent tickled Hannah's nostrils. However, she refused to sneeze and break the moment.

She wiggled her nose but otherwise didn't move. "I didn't want to believe it when Derek told me. I thought that surely you wouldn't keep something that big from me for all these years. But it's true, isn't it?"

"Hannah, sit down." Her father attempted an authoritative tone, one that would have made her immediately plop into a chair a few days ago, but today his voice faltered.

Her mother darted her gaze from her father to the floor, then to Hannah for a brief moment and finally to the door out of the room. "Shall I call for some tea? Maybe a ginger ale, dear?" She plucked a tissue from a hidden pocket and dabbed at her eyes.

Hannah forced herself to suck in a deep breath before she answered. "No, thank you, Mother. I don't need anything to drink. I need answers."

Her mother half collapsed on a floral, upholstered fainting couch. "Of course."

"Evelyn." It was a warning tone. A be-quiet-and-I'll-handle-this tone. Her father turned to her, a distinct lack of confidence surrounding him. "Hannah, you are our daughter, and we love you. That is the truth. Isn't that all you need to know?"

"I don't doubt that you love me. But I want to know why you never told me I was adopted."

"Fine." He closed the heavy oak doors to the den and then returned to stand in front of Hannah and Derek, gesturing to the sofa. "If you insist. But please, let's all sit down."

He moved a wingback chair close to Hannah's mother, who had managed to sit upright on the couch. She grasped his hand as if it was a life preserver and tumultuous waves were about to overcome her. "I presume you want Derek here?"

How could he ask such a thing? She had brought him, hadn't she? She had never been rebellious, but this was almost too much. She had a sudden urge to grab Derek's hand, but that could send a signal she didn't intend. Her teeth ground together as she forced out one word. "Yes."

A long moment stretched between them, gathering among them and gaining strength until Hannah wondered if the silence would ever be broken.

Eventually, her father drew a breath and spoke quietly as he stared at the floor. "As you know now, you are adopted."

So there it was. True, she hadn't quite believed Derek. Something that big and life-altering she needed to hear from the very people who had made it happen. She sat motionless, afraid that any small movement would bring further catastrophe into her world. She fixed her gaze on the Renoir reproduction on the far wall—a little girl holding a water can, gazing solemnly outside of the photo. If she sat as still as that painted little girl, would her life stop changing?

Her throat closed up and she couldn't manage a single word to her father or mother.

"Hannah, darling, please let us explain the circumstances."

A large, warm hand grasped hers, strength flowing from Derek to her. The pounding of her heart slowed slightly, but the pressure on her chest remained constant. She squeezed his hand, an attempt to convey gratitude at his presence.

Her father rearranged himself on the chair, as if a new position would make the conversation more comfortable. "Hannah, the world was a different place twenty-five years ago. You'll think I'm selfish for keeping the truth from you, that we are selfish—" he nodded toward his wife "—but please hear me out before you come to any conclusions about us. I've thought on this many times over the years, and there are three main reasons.

"First, adoption has never been looked kindly upon in our social circles. You know the business I built from the ground up. You know the networking that's required for success. The country club. Your mother's social activities with the wives of my business associates. You are not our child by blood, and our social acquaintances would view us differently. We loved you and wanted you to be a part of our family, but we couldn't stand to tell anyone because we would lose our social standing."

Her mother dabbed at another tear. "Adoptive parents, then, weren't the heroes they are now."

Hannah couldn't say she liked their reasoning, but she understood it. The people she knew from her parents' connections could not be relied upon to be kind and understanding. "Okay. Your second reason?"

"You, dear."

Her father stroked her mother's hand and let her choke out a sob before he resumed the explanation. "We wanted to protect you within our social circles. You know their character, or lack thereof. We've tried to instill in you kindness and generosity and many characteristics that come from faith that so many of them do not possess because of their lack of faith. And many of our friends, if you choose to call them that, can be downright cruel. We didn't want them to think less of you. To see you as an orphan or a reject. Or worse yet, for you to be bullied and made an outcast."

Hannah felt her arms and legs relax slightly, and she inhaled a deep, cleansing breath. Her parents had a point. Despite their affluence, or perhaps because of it, her own social circle at the private school had been riddled with bullies. Peer pressure was fierce, and many afternoons she had rushed home, escaped to her own room and pacified herself with classical music, a good book and sometimes a piece of chocolate.

Her parents stared at her, her mother with one hand open on her lap, as if seeking a reassurance that their relationship with their daughter was not lost. "I think I'm understanding your reasons, Mother and Father, but it's not easy. You said you had three?"

"Yes. You'll be curious about your birth mother. Perhaps someday you'll wonder about your birth father. But we have no idea who she was or where she is now. Our final reason for not telling you is because the lawyer that called me about your availability advised us that you not be told you were adopted for your own protection. Those were his exact words."

A shiver raced down her spine. "I am curious about my birth mother, but I already know about my birth father. According to Derek, he's part of an organized crime family." She darted her gaze to the French doors that led to a large patio and the landscaped yard and pool. "And it seems that he's trying to find me. To hurt me." The very thought pierced her heart with terror.

Derek squeezed her hand again. She startled, having completely forgotten that he was there, comforting her, reassuring her. She jerked her stare to him. "That's why Derek is here."

"Sweetheart." Her mother's gentle tone drew Hannah back to the conversation. "We didn't know what that lawyer meant. No one told us about your birth parents. But it scared us. Still, we loved you. Adored you. And we figured you would have a better life with us, even without knowing the truth, than you would have had in whatever dangerous situation your birth mother was in."

"I hope you can understand and forgive us," her father said. "His words scared us. We were worried for you. For all of us. So we haven't even breathed a word of it to each other for nearly twenty-five years."

Her parents certainly seemed genuine in what they were saying. Hannah watched carefully and didn't see any sign of deception. Just real worry.

She blinked slowly to clear her vision, to try to see more clearly. Love was shining in the countenances of both of her parents as her father nodded to her mother.

Her mother rose steadily from the couch. "Hannah, I have something you need to see."

Derek squeezed her hand and released it. "I'll be right here." He touched his hand to the outside of his shirt, where his holster rested. A signal that he would stay with her. Protect her.

They left the den and turned down the hallway and up the stairs. Hannah looked at all the furnishings and accoutrements of her family home with a new vision, as if seeing the knickknacks and photos with a clearer understanding. Inside the master suite, a well-appointed grouping of rooms decorated with delicate pinks and greens, Hannah's mother led her into her inner sanctum, a space that Hannah had only been allowed into a handful of times. A sitting area sat past an ornate mirror that went from floor to ceiling. A glance into the mirror revealed a young woman with brows creased together and lips compressed into a tight line. Hannah stopped to look more closely. Was that really her, with that tired, stricken look?

"Hannah," her mother called softly. Tenderly. The voice of a mother protecting and nurturing her child. "Sit here." She gestured to a pink-and-white upholstered chair.

Hannah obediently sat, the numbness that had crept over her showing no signs of dissipating. Her mother curled her fingers under the right edge of the mirror and pulled. It opened like a door.

She disappeared inside for a few minutes, then reappeared holding an envelope and sat in a chair that matched Hannah's. "I have something here that I've had since I first held you in my arms. Your father and I contemplated, once upon a time, destroying it as a means of protecting you. As a way to hide whatever identity you had before you came to us. But we never could. It always seemed that it belonged more to you than to us. So we held on to it, hoping and praying that there would never be occasion to retrieve it." She stopped to take a deep breath, loosened her clutch on the envelope and color returned to her fingernails.

Hannah couldn't think of a single thing to say.

Her mother held out the envelope, and Hannah grasped it, laying it in her lap. "I don't know what is in this envelope. I've never opened it. But it has your name on it. If I was your birth mother, giving you up to another, I would write a letter to you. That may be what this is."

Hannah broke eye contact with her mother and stared at the envelope. Would it reveal secrets she was suddenly desperate for? Or would it simply raise more questions?

Hannah and her mother sat in awkward silence. What could she say now? It seemed there was nothing to be said. Her mother seemed to be sharing everything she knew, and up until today, she had never known her mother to be anything other than completely honest. There was no reason to doubt her now.

Dryness threatened her throat, and Hannah swallowed hard. "Thank you," she whispered. She stood and rushed from the room.

"Hannah," her mother called from behind her, out in the hallway, but she needed a moment alone to read whatever was in that envelope.

Back in the den, she beelined toward the French doors that opened onto the large patio. She met Derek's questioning gaze and nodded for him to follow. Outside, she leaned a hand on a stone column, and took several gulps of fresh air, hoping to steady her nerves. Derek closed the doors gently behind them. He walked around to stand next to her, at a distance close enough to be comforting but not so close as to intrude on her space. It was just the right angle to protect her from the wide open backyard.

She straightened and paced down the stone steps and around the large pool surrounded by boulders and willowy reeds and flower beds. A covered seating area with a sofa and wrought-iron armchairs tastefully arranged on a blue-and-white outdoor rug in front of a large fireplace beckoned her, and Derek followed. His presence soothed her somewhat, but she was still a bundle of nerves.

She held the envelope out to show him. "Mother just gave me this. I don't know what's in it yet, but I didn't want to open it in front of them." The sofa called to her, to collapse into it, to pull the gauzy curtains around the comfortable space and block out the world. But she couldn't seem to stop pacing.

Without a word, Derek stood in front of

her, gently maneuvering her into the back recesses of the patio.

She nodded her assent, then slid a quivering finger under the envelope flap. Inside was a single piece of paper. Hannah withdrew it and opened it to find the name of a ritzy downtown Chicago hotel embossed at the top. A practiced and careful script filled the rest of the page.

My dearest darling daughter,
If you are reading this, it means you now know that you are adopted. Please know that it was my wish that you not be told. I knew that you would be better off with a loving and caring adoptive family who could provide safety and stability and normalcy for you in a way that I never could have.

My relationship with your father was brief. I loved him, but then I found God's love, and my life was never the same. I prayed for your father. I begged him to give up his evil ways and live a life pleasing to God. I won't go into detail, but I was forced to run for my life. I kept you for as long as I could, but ultimately, the only sure way to save you was to give you up. I can leave you with only two things. First, this letter that I pray assures you of my love. And second, your most beloved doll with the carnation-pink dress and the brown yarn hair. Please keep them both safe.

I long to hold you, to wipe away the tears you may shed when you read this, to tell you with my own voice how much I love you. But for your benefit, I cannot reveal myself to you, and I beg you not to search for me.

I would give my life for you.

Susan

At the sight of her birth mother's name, Hannah's tears erupted. She thrust the letter at Derek, and he came to her, grasping the letter with one hand and encircling her waist with his free arm. She sank into his chest, letting her tears be absorbed by his T-shirt as she thanked the Lord for the strength of his arm around her.

So that was all she was going to get? Despite how much her sense of identity, even the foundation of her family, had changed in the last few hours, she still didn't know much. Her mother's name was Susan, and at one point, she had been in Chicago. Something terrible had happened that made her think that Hannah was safest without her. But what? And whatever it was, was it coming back now to harm her?

She tore away from Derek. His comfort had been helpful for the moment, but there was no point in relying on him. He was only here temporarily. She couldn't count on him for the long term, so there was no reason to depend on him now.

Suddenly, the comfortable and quiet life of garden-club meetings and country-club tennis looked wonderful. Her parents had provided so, so much for her that she had taken for granted growing up. Yet, a secret had been withheld from her. The very nature of her identity. Why she didn't look like anyone in the family. Why she had always felt a little bit like an outsider, even in what she had thought was her home environment. Why her interests and pursuits had been so different from everyone else's.

Derek's quiet tone broke into her reverie, diffusing what had been becoming a build-up of anger and resentment. "Your birth mother mentioned a doll. Do you still have it?"

The doll. Hannah mentally raced through

the few boxes of childhood keepsakes she had stashed in the back of her closet. "Yes. Father thought I should get rid of it along with many other things from my childhood. But it was one of my favorites. It's tucked away in my closet." She had to find it. If it was important to her birth mother then it was important to her. "Stay here. I'll be right back."

She dashed back through the den, down the hallway and into her old bedroom. With a few minutes of rifling through boxes at the back of the closet, she found the doll. As she emerged from the closet, her gaze fell on the now-empty window seat in her room. As she had packed for her move to her apartment, she had taken one last photo of her mementos arranged on the seat, things she loved but just couldn't take with her. That photo had appeared on her blog along with a post about packing away the old to make room for the new. A couple of her friends had shared online their own photos of keepsakes they couldn't let go of. It had been encouraging at the time, knowing she wasn't alone in her sentiments or in keeping boxes of childhood reminders.

But now a moment of apprehension stopped her. She pulled out her phone to see the photo again, the photo she had plastered all over her online world. The doll's blue eyes seemed to twinkle at her and the yarn mouth smiled encouragement and love as Hannah closed the bedroom door behind her, doll in hand, eager to return to Derek and what felt like safety.

Back on the patio, she handed it to Derek. He turned it all around, examining it, then handed it back. "Do you have any memory of being with another family?"

"Not at all. I don't remember anything but Mother and Father."

"Then you must have been quite young when they got you. Probably under two years old." He stepped closer and touched the doll's hair where some yarn was coming loose from the seam. "She must have been a great comfort to you."

"Yes. I guess it's just part of my personality to keep things. I can't part with keepsakes that have meant so much to me." How surreal. A younger version of herself had probably clutched this dolly to her chest as she met her new mommy and daddy, yet this older version who held it now had no recollection whatsoever of those exact moments. Whatever had happened in the past, Hannah only knew that she felt a sense of security when she held the doll.

She tore her gaze from the rag doll and looked up into the rich brown eyes of this living, breathing man in front of her. He was definitely real, and she had plenty of memories of him. "What do I do now?"

"First, you remember that you should lean on God. He is your defender and your protector. He's in all of this, and none of it is a surprise to Him."

"Yes, you're right. Of course."

Derek stepped closer and laid his hands on her arms, his touch warming her in the cool of the early summer evening. "He protected you as a child. The letter reads like your birth mother found the Lord, accepted His salvation and knew that the best she could do for you was to give you to the safety of a loving family."

Her mind tried to wrap around that thought, despite the distraction of Derek's nearness. Questions and desires and doubts assaulted her.

A loud crack broke the stillness of the moment. Glass shattered behind her.

Someone was shooting at them!

Derek pulled her to the ground. Her hip hit

the cement slab, cushioned only by the thin rug. She winced and kept her eyes closed as he rolled with her farther into the sitting area. Pain shot down her leg. She longed to massage it, but she held on to Derek tightly instead. The air around her seemed suddenly still, and she sucked in a breath, mentally running over her arms and legs. She wasn't shot, and Derek seemed to be in one piece as well.

In one fluid motion, he lifted himself from her and grabbed his weapon from the holster hidden under his shirt. His eyes were trained on the landscaping across a grassy area.

"Hannah!" Her father's strident tone brought her focus to the back of the house, and she propped herself up on an elbow. "Come inside!"

Her father stood to the side of a French door that now had a jagged hole in the middle. Her mother seemed to tremble several feet behind, her cell phone in her hand, probably—hopefully—calling 911.

"Father, get back!" she squeaked out, but she doubted that he could hear her.

A second shot suddenly struck the back of a wrought-iron chair just inches from her. Derek, crouching low, pushed her down in front of the massive stone fireplace. "Who is it?" she whispered.

Derek didn't remove his gaze from the landscaping. "Not sure. I can only see the shrubs moving."

Hannah huddled down, a quiet prayer escaping her lips—she was grateful for her protector. She had heard, over the years, that Derek had joined the police force, but she hadn't seen him since high school and hadn't known, until that day, that he was FBI. Hadn't seen him wield his weapon. Hadn't seen his training in action. It was an impressive thing to behold.

"Let's go." He gestured toward the bushes that ran alongside the pool. "Follow me, close to the house, and stay low."

"What about my parents?" She couldn't leave them in danger.

"They've called for police. I'll get the guy if I can, but my first responsibility is to protect you." He nodded. "Now let's go."

With his weapon still in hand, he crawled from behind the fireplace into the bushes near the pool. Hannah stared at the house. Her father and mother had retreated and couldn't be seen from her vantage point. But how could she leave them?

"Hannah." The urgent whisper came from ahead. Derek was now several feet in front of her. She didn't want to leave, but she needed to trust him. He had the weapon and, it seemed, more knowledge of her situation than she did.

Balling her crinkled skirt into one fist to make crawling easier, she inched out from behind the fireplace and in the direction Derek was headed. She glanced back toward the house and saw her parents crouched down behind the curtain, watching Derek and then her crawl away. Her father had retrieved his own weapon, probably from some hidden safe, but he held it at his side, perhaps unable to clearly see the man who threatened them. Her heart broke for her parents. She couldn't imagine what they must be feeling, after the confrontation they had just had about her adoption, and then watching some thug shoot at their only daughter. Now she was leaving them behind with so much unsettled between them.

A flutter of the bushes ahead caught her attention, and she riveted her gaze back to Derek. It was best that she focus on getting out alive. She sped up her crawl until she was within a couple of feet of his shoes.

As he neared the far edge of the pool, almost to the point where they could make a run out of the backyard, the bushes parted. A tall, burly man leaped out toward Derek, a blur moving so quickly she couldn't distinguish his facial features. Derek must have seen him coming, for he lunged upward toward the man's chest, and loud *oompfs* erupted from both of them.

Without assessing the risk to her or to Derek, Hannah sprang up and ran forward, picking up as much speed as she could in the few feet between them. The element of surprise was on her side as the man stepped away from Derek, his arm raised as if to swing it at him. He spied her and seemed frozen for the moment it took for Hannah to close the space between them. Leading with her shoulder, she rammed him in the upper abdomen. Her momentum continued a couple more steps until he stumbled backward. His heel hit the low curb that surrounded the landscaping around the pool. Arms flailing, his weapon flew out of his hand and into the far shrubbery. A loud splash heralded his fall into the pool, and cool drops of water splashed on Hannah's nose and cheeks and forehead.

Derek grabbed her hand, and she glanced

over at him, her efforts rewarded with his wide smile. "Come on, GI Jane."

Without letting go of his grasp, she followed him around the pool. A glance over her shoulder revealed the thug floundering in the water, as if he couldn't swim. If he would just put his feet down, that was the shallow end. But she wasn't going to give him any pointers. Over her other shoulder, she saw her parents step out of the house, her father training his weapon on the shooter.

Her father shot a look at her, making eye contact. "Hannah! Come back here with us for your protection."

But Derek tugged on her hand and her heart. With whom should she go?

The pressure of Hannah's hand in his reinforced Derek's resolve to keep her safe no matter what. The thug still seemed to be stuck in the pool, and even if he got out before they got away, his weapon was lost in the bushes. It didn't seem likely that he had any other weapon on him since he hadn't retrieved it yet. And Mr. and Mrs. McClarnon would be safe until the police arrived. Even now, sirens began to pierce the air.

Mr. McClarnon kept his gun focused on the

pool, but he followed after them a few steps. "Hannah, come back. It's safer. The police are almost here."

Derek could feel Hannah slowing, her steps lagging behind, her hand slipping out of his. There might be only one thug this time, but there would be more later, and her father wasn't trained and didn't have the maneuvers to protect her against these guys who killed whenever it suited their purposes. Now was the time to reveal himself to Hannah's parents.

He pulled the badge from his belt and held it high so they could see it in the evening twilight. The pool lights reflected off the brass. "I'm FBI now, Mr. McClarnon. Hannah will definitely be safer with me."

The older man gasped loudly, the lights from the house illuminating the shock etched on his face. He had always underestimated Derek, but Derek didn't have the time or the inclination to revel in the bump-up of respect that, most likely, he had just achieved. Protecting Hannah was his number-one priority.

Without taking his eyes off the man in the pool, Derek nodded to Hannah. "Stay low."

He retrieved the handcuffs from his belt and fished the thug out of the water, wrestling him onto the grass and securing him as soon as he was facedown on solid ground. "What's your name? Who do you work for?" Derek didn't expect any answers, but now was the best time to get him to talk, before he had time to think or contact his lawyer.

The man didn't answer, just spit out a bit of pool water and grass.

"Who else is with you?"

No answer.

"What do you want?"

Derek only got a grunt from the man.

The sirens approached quickly, and soon the backyard was filled with a half-dozen uniformed officers. He filled them in and left the thug in the capable hands of the police. He wasn't going to answer any of Derek's questions anyway.

Derek grabbed Hannah's hand again, and they darted around the side of the house. He released her hand at the car, too worried until now that she might run back to what she thought was the safe sanctuary of her parents' home. She slid in to the passenger side, lines of concern creasing around her eyes and furrowing through her forehead as she tucked the letter and the doll into the bag she had left in the vehicle. A lot had happened today, and Derek would take it all away if he could. But the best he could do now was protect and comfort.

Comfort carefully, so as to keep his emotional distance.

He turned the Escape around in the wide driveway, tires squealing and a faint stench of burning rubber wafting into the SUV. At the end of the McClarnons' lane, he turned away from the police vehicles with lights still flashing parked at the front of the house. He drove carefully and counted the cars as they passed. Three police vehicles and an ambulance sat at the mansion. Assured that the McClarnons would be well cared for, he turned his attention back to the road ahead.

The short hairs on the back of his neck tickled, and he turned to find Hannah staring at him, questions and concerns narrowing her pretty brown eyes. "Why are we driving away from Mother and Father?" She crossed her arms across her seat belt.

Law school had certainly taught her a few things about cross examination.

"First of all, your parents will be safer if we lure any other bad guys away. They don't want your parents. Second, you saw all those police officers. The thug is in custody. Your parents are fine."

"My parents have an alarm that alerts them when anyone comes onto the property. Why didn't they hear it?"

That was a concern and something Derek should pass on to his supervising agent. "I don't know exactly. We can't rule out a simple malfunction. But it could be that that guy disabled it in some way."

"So they're smart bad guys?"

"Most are."

She scowled at him. "That's not comforting."

"We just need to be smarter."

Hannah's cell phone trilled, and Mrs. McClarnon's face appeared on the screen. Hannah answered it on speaker. "Mother? Are you all right?"

"Yes, darling. Your father and I are fine physically." Her voice wavered a bit. "It's been quite an ordeal for one day. I have wondered if this day would come, the day we would need to tell you the truth. Yet I never imagined it would include a strange man nearly drowning in our pool and a bullet through our French doors."

"Mrs. McClarnon, have the police been

able to get any information out of him?"
Derek hoped Hannah and her mother didn't
mind his intrusion on their call, but the more
he knew about the attacker, the more he could
report to his superior.

"Oh, Derek? What a blessing that you were
here to protect us all. Thank you."

"You're welcome, ma'am. I'm glad no one
was hurt."

"I'm not so sure about Mr. McClarnon. He
was worried about what the neighbors might
think with our home surrounded by law-enforcement vehicles. Then, when they got out
the yellow tape to mark off the crime scene,
he almost collapsed. The officer who seemed
to be in charge insisted that it at least go in
the backyard."

Derek glanced to check Hannah's expression in time to see a half-suppressed eye roll,
her lips pressed tightly together. Everyone had
different priorities, and they could switch in
an instant, depending on the circumstances.
During the shooting, Mr. McClarnon's priority was the safety of his family—his wife and
daughter—and perhaps even Derek. But once
the area was secure again, he reverted back to
his old ways. A man didn't get ahead in business without some concern for what others

thought. That wasn't the way Derek wanted to live his own life, but to each his own.

"Mrs. McClarnon, that's fine. They just want to keep people out of the area until they're done sweeping for evidence. Anything that might help them figure out who that perp is and why he was there." Derek doubted the police would find anything but some damaged shrubbery, but it was important that the McClarnons let law enforcement do their job. "They won't take long."

"Mother?" Hannah broke in. "You never said if the police know the man's name."

"Oh, that's right. No, dear. He hasn't said a word, and they've taken him now." A sigh slipped through the phone. "Please be careful, sweetheart. Stay with Derek. He'll protect you in whatever is going on."

"Yes, Mother." She said goodbye then ended the call.

Well, he had one parent's approval. It could be just temporary, until their daughter was safe again. But for now, Derek wanted to puff out his chest in victory. Maybe he had something to contribute after all.

"So they're fine. All's well that ends well. What now?"

Derek admired the beautiful smile that lit

Hannah's face, but her eyes were wide and worry tinged her cheerful tone. She had always been happy and kind and generous, all qualities that had drawn Derek to her in the first place. But it hadn't taken too many conversations to realize that her smile didn't always reach her heart. Her smile hid her discomfort in different situations. Often, the bigger the smile, Derek knew, the greater her discomfort.

Right now, her smile was ginormous.

Yes, she had reason to be relieved. A shooter had come onto her parents' property, into the privacy of their backyard, and tried to shoot her and harm him. They had come out of it triumphant, albeit temporarily. But this was nowhere near the end of it, and judging by her body language, Hannah was hiding a load of anxiety.

"Now, we need another vehicle. This Escape would give us away. We need something entirely different." He turned onto the highway that had brought them to the McClarnons' and headed back into Lafayette. "I saw a rental car agency back by the funeral home, the same agency chain I got this SUV from. We'll stop there and trade it in for something else."

"Fine. And then what?" She shot him a glare, and he squirmed in his seat. She would make a good lawyer someday very soon.

"Then we find someplace safe."

It didn't take long at the rental agency to trade the Escape for a Toyota Corolla in blue crush metallic. Hannah gushed over the color before he ushered her into her seat and closed the door. He stepped a few paces from the car to check up and down the street, but it didn't appear that they had been followed. Now, if that thug's cohorts came looking for the Escape, they would reach a dead end.

As he slid into the driver's seat, his phone jabbed him, a reminder that he needed to call his supervising agent and report the shooting. He would want to be involved in the questioning of the perp. Derek closed the driver-side door, and the intoxicating floral scent of Hannah's perfume or shampoo or whatever it was—just her sweet essence, maybe—assaulted him.

"Does this car remind you of something?" Hannah turned to him. There was no twinkle in her eye, no smile crinkling her nose, but she was ready to lead him through a memory. She probably didn't want to think about

their situation anymore, and this would provide a distraction. That was fine for her, but a
distraction for him could be deadly for them
both. He twitched his nose and shook his head
to clear out all other thoughts than keeping
her safe.

"No." He turned the key in the ignition and
gripped the steering wheel, figuring he ought
to play along. "Should it?"

"The car you drove in high school." She
spoke in a matter-of-fact tone.

"What? I drove a 1990 black Pontiac Grand
Am. This one's blue, in much better shape,
and has an entirely different interior." She
must be really worried if she was grasping
for memories.

"Okay, but it still reminds me of your old
car. You there and me here. Out for a drive."

"I can't believe that old Grand Am drove as
well as it did. It was a good car but the previ-
ous owner obviously hadn't been kind to it."
He chuckled ruefully. "It had flooded some
time before I got it and, although I cleaned
it up as best I could, it was still just a heap
of junk after sixteen years. But it was the
only one I could afford with my five hundred dollars from shoveling snow and mow-
ing lawns."

"We had some good times in it, driving to get ice cream, having deep philosophical discussions."

"At least as deep and philosophical as teenagers can get. I remember mostly complaining about the amount of homework." Too much homework had kept him from having more time with her.

Hannah clasped her hands together in her lap. "Weren't we foolish? Was complaining just a state of mind? We got our diplomas, went on to college and look at us now."

Derek checked the rearview mirror as he gained speed, just like he needed to speed out of her life after this assignment was completed. He had wanted to go to the same college as Hannah, continue their relationship and not have to hide it. But then Mr. McClarnon had told him to stay away, and he had opted for community college in another town. By the time he had returned to Heartwood Hill, the McClarnons had moved their business and their home to Lafayette.

In hindsight, he and Hannah had been foolish. Foolish to fall in love. Foolish to think that they might have had a future together.

Hannah's soft voice broke into his thoughts, but she spoke as though she didn't realize he could hear her. "We had some good times together."

Derek pressed a hand to his chest, trying to still his increased heart rate. He remembered those moments well. But now?

Hannah had made it clear that she would rather be an unmarried lawyer than marry a young man from her social circle. And Derek had been told in no uncertain terms that he didn't belong anywhere near that social circle. Besides, he had a great career ahead of him with the FBI. His dream job. Neither of them was in the market for a relationship. Not with each other. Not with anyone.

Case closed.

They drove in silence for several minutes. Derek took the opportunity to pray for God's wisdom in his first assignment and for Hannah to understand and accept her adoption, trusting the Lord to make His will known.

He also called Square and apprised him of the events that had unfolded at the McClarnon mansion. Hannah was still secure, although Derek was disappointed that he couldn't identify their attacker. The agent praised his work and cautioned him to stay safe and keep checking in.

Hannah was still quiet, and he thought she

was praying as well, until she turned toward him. "I know what to do next. Find out more about the circumstances of my birth. Then find my birth mother."

FIVE

Hannah pulled her hair across her cheek, twisting her finger in it, surreptitiously watching Derek as he steered the Corolla onto the interstate. He had matured well, and he was definitely a handsome man, turning heads wherever they went. But he had changed in the ten years since she'd known him. He was hardened. Not exactly stoic, but unmoving and less tender than he had been with her. Maybe it was his law-enforcement background. Maybe it was the end of their relationship. Maybe he was still sweet underneath the tough exterior, but he just refused to let it out. He was on the job, after all.

And that's all she was to him now. A job. An assignment.

That was good, right?

Derek settled the vehicle into the middle lane behind a large semi, then punctured her with a sideways look. "What do you mean, find your birth mother?"

She tapped on her phone to bring up Google, then entered a search for the *Chicago Tribune* around her birth date. "My birth mother was in danger. She gave me up to keep me safe from somebody. Maybe there was something reported about whatever happened to her. I'm searching the archives of the *Tribune* to see if there are any articles." She scrolled down the pages of the newspaper. "I'm just glad it's online. I wasn't sure what I would find."

He drove in silence for a couple of miles, then asked, "Anything?"

"Nothing. Maybe a smaller community newspaper? You said the FBI had a man on the inside of the crime family. Where are they located?"

"All over the place. And we don't know where the event that culminated in your adoption took place. Do you know the names of any of the smaller newspapers?"

She stared out the window. "No." Were they at a dead end before they'd even begun?

"What about a general Google search for newspapers in the Chicago area?"

"Yeah, that should work." She tapped again,

and soon a list of less than a half-dozen newspapers came up, complete with links. But when she clicked through, the websites didn't provide any archives. "I found some newspaper names, but the online issues don't go back far enough. Are they too small to be completely digital?"

"Maybe. We've become so accustomed to everything being available online, I'm not sure how to search next."

Hannah laid her phone in her lap. "The public library. With my librarian friend, Tallulah."

"I know you want more information, Hannah. I'm curious, too. But my assignment is to keep you safe."

"Good. I appreciate that," she retorted. "But you can keep me safe at the public library, can't you? It's public. Lots of people."

"Well, the library in downtown Indianapolis would be quite a distance from both your parents' house and the offices in Heartwood Hill. I suppose it could be a good place to hide out for a while." He clicked on the turn signal and moved into the right lane.

"The way I see it is that I have the most to lose. That makes me the most motivated to figure out what's going on. I can't just sit

around and wait for news. I need to do something. To feel productive. I need to find my
birth mother, or at least find out what happened to her. That could lead us to know for
sure who's been shooting at me." While they
were stuck in the car together, she would continue her direct examination. There was no
place for him to go or hide. "How much does
the FBI know about our past?"

"I was assigned to you because I'm from
Heartwood Hill. They thought that my knowledge of the area might give me an advantage."
He paused. "My supervising agent knows that
we were friends in high school. That's it."

"Oh."

"I'd just completed the academy and ex-
pressed my interest in investigating organized
crime. Now, I'm here."

"Why organized crime?"

He scrubbed a hand over his chin. Something difficult was coming, and Hannah
wanted to put a comforting hand on his arm.
She fisted her hand instead, to keep it in her
lap.

"You know I was raised by my aunt and
uncle, right? My parents died when I was a
teenager."

"Yes, you told me that much in high school.

That's how you came to be in Heartwood Hill. You never explained anything further."

"My parents were killed in a shootout. They were caught in what was believed to be a Mafia hit." A vein ticked in his temple. It was a distressing memory for him, of that Hannah was sure.

"Mafia? Are you sure?"

"Yes. The facts don't lie."

"I'm so sorry, Derek. That's just…awful." So that was it. Derek wanted to right the wrong of his parents' murders by fighting organized crime with the FBI. But a fresh tremor of fear for her situation struck her with the word *Mafia*.

She hugged her arms tight around her middle, not caring that the seat belt was cutting into her neck. From what little she knew of the Mafia, they had nearly unlimited resources. She flipped the visor down to look behind them in the vanity mirror. Was anyone following? Surely Derek would monitor that. He had said that he would keep her safe. But she couldn't just wait for strangers to straighten out the mess that her life had become.

"Well, given the present circumstances, wouldn't it be helpful to know why I wasn't safe before, and why I'm apparently not safe now? Plus, if my birth mother is still alive after all these years, she's probably in danger as well. We need to get to the library and start researching ASAP." Tallulah would know what to do.

Derek sighed. "Well, I suppose it couldn't hurt. And if we find anything, it might be helpful to the investigation." He pulled into the exit lane for Meridian Street and headed south toward the main branch of the public library.

"Thank you." This time, Hannah did lay her hand on his forearm and immediately regretted it as warmth flowed through her and a fierce pang of longing shot straight to her heart.

The public library was a monstrous structure of stone and glass, six stories of stacks of books and study tables and private carrels. It was the perfect place to hide. It had been when they were in high school, studying on a Friday night, and Hannah couldn't think of a reason why it wouldn't be now.

Every inch of Derek seemed on alert as he pulled into the underground parking garage and craned his neck to look in all directions. Hannah glanced around as well, but all seemed secure. Besides, who would dare to attack them in such a public place?

The elevator deposited them on the first floor, and Hannah made straight for the reference desk. Tallulah stood behind it, but she was turned to the side, on the telephone.

"You still come here?" Derek kept his voice low in respect of the other patrons.

"Every Friday night. It's been a practice and I just can't see any reason to stop." Her palms slicked against her skirt, and she swallowed down a sensation she hadn't felt in a while. Not since the last time, years ago, when Derek had walked into the library by her side. It had been the last time she had ever spent any quality time with him. They had graduated a couple of weeks later, and she had seen him on the other side of the crowd. But then he had disappeared. "I study. I read. I wander the stacks and run my hands over the book spines. They have a little coffee shop now, so sometimes I have a coffee with Tallulah."

"Who's this Tallulah you keep mentioning?"

"She's a reference librarian and also an adjunct professor at the law school. She teaches legal research and writing. I can't tell you what a blessing it's been to know her. I suppose she's a kind of mentor." Hannah hitched her purse higher on her shoulder. "Actually, Tallulah is a big part of why I wanted to go to law school. She made the law sound fascinating, each person and each case as a story to be read, analyzed and applied."

Derek halted in the middle of the oversized dome-shaped foyer, his shoulders stiffening and his shoes squeaking softly on the floor as he turned in a three-sixty. Hannah pulled up short to stand next to him. "What is it?"

"It's been a long time since I've been in here. Brings back a lot of memories."

"Yes." There didn't seem to be anything else to say. She reached for his hand, and he held it as they stood together, looking around. When she had begun law school and returned to their Friday-night study habit, memories had flooded her. Her heart had agonized over the loss of him every single Friday until she thought she couldn't come any longer. But eventually, the sensation wore off. She had forced herself to push thoughts of him aside and focus on her legal studies. Tallulah's friendship had helped.

"I always thought of the library as ground zero for our relationship."

"How so?"

"This was our home base. Our hideout. Our starting point. If we had studied in Heartwood Hill, we would have seen people we knew, and everything would have come out. And if we ever did reveal ourselves, there would have been an explosion."

Hannah bit the inside of her cheek, pondering what he'd just said. *Had* there been an explosion that she didn't know about? Was that why Derek had disappeared?

Tallulah spotted them and waved. Hannah quickly slipped her hand from his and waved back. Whatever had caused their breakup, she wouldn't be able to discover it now. One shooter had been apprehended at her parents' house, but there could be other men who would come for them soon enough. The FBI hadn't told Derek that they were out of danger. That was the more immediate concern.

"Well, well." Tallulah eyed Derek up and down, a knowing look marching across her countenance. "It's not Friday yet, is it?"

"Not yet, but we need to do some research." Hannah leaned on the counter.

"Glad to see it's *we* again."

Furrowing his brow, Derek shifted his balance next to Hannah. "What do you mean?"

Tallulah clicked her nails on the desk. "Oh,

I was here. How many years has it been? Nearly ten? But I saw you every Friday night. You just didn't notice me, because you only had eyes for each other." A sly smile slid across her mouth.

A pink haze began to spread up Derek's neck, and Hannah figured she had a matching shade. She had had no idea that anyone had noticed them. Tallulah winked at Hannah, sending her the full force of her knowing grin.

Words failed both of them as awkwardness invaded, but Tallulah seemed pleased as Punch. She shifted to pick up a stack of hardback books. "I have the books you were asking about a couple of weeks ago."

"Since I'm on summer break, I wanted to read some legal suspense." Hannah turned to Derek, eager to switch gears. "Tallulah was kind enough to find the bestselling authors for me."

"Good."

The librarian handed the thick tomes to Hannah. "They're already checked out to your account."

"Thank you. But what we really need is help with some research. We're looking for news from the Chicago area from about twenty-five years ago. I found the *Tribune* online but couldn't get any of the smaller papers."

After one long look at the two of them, Tallulah came from behind the counter. "Sure. That'll be in the basement."

A long flight of wide steps led them to the lower level, a cavernous space with deep red carpeting, more book stacks and long rows of partitioned desks. Lamps stood sentinel along the desks, a few turned on but most of them dark. It could have been cozy if it wasn't so creepy.

The librarian led them to a wooden table with a microfilm reader. "Because of your time frame, you're finding some newspapers digitally. Others you'll have to find on microfilm. About twenty-five years ago, newspapers began creating their copy digitally. If the copy was created originally in digital form, then it's easy to get online. If it wasn't, you'll have to find it the old-fashioned way. On microfilm. Getting older newspapers in digital format is time-consuming and expensive. Obviously, that's easier for the big papers like the *Tribune* than for the small papers with a more limited budget."

"Okay. If we each search the various Chicago papers, it'll go faster."

"Sounds like a plan." Tallulah gestured toward drawers labeled with various years. "These are filled with microfilm of original newspapers. Since Chicago is so close, we have all the editions. They're in chronological order, of course." She turned to Derek. "Why don't you get started here, and I'll show Hannah how to use the reader."

He nodded and studied the years on the drawer labels.

The microfilm reader was several steps away, and as Hannah sat, Tallulah leaned over and whispered in her ear. "You don't seem yourself. Distracted. A little nervous. Is everything okay?"

What should she say? Hannah desperately wanted to honor her mother and father. They obviously hadn't wanted anyone to know she was adopted, and she wanted to abide by their wishes. But also, if she told, would Tallulah be in danger then as well? She definitely didn't want to put the librarian in the line of fire.

"Life is a little hectic right now. And more than a little confusing." She cut her eyes toward Derek. All that was certainly true enough.

Tallulah stared at her for a long moment. "All right. But whatever is going on, don't forget to lean on God. Trust Him, for He will take care of you. Both of you."

"I know. But thanks for the reminder."

"I'll pray for the two of you to find God's way through whatever it is."

"Thank you."

With a few quick instructions, Tallulah left them to their research. Hannah looked around the basement. No one else was around, and surely there was no way they could be found down there. It was a terrific hiding spot. As Derek shuffled through film on his reader a few feet away, she studied articles from around the time of her birth.

What would have been the circumstances where her safety, as a baby, was in jeopardy? What kind of a man was her birth father if he truly had wanted to harm her? Or did he want to harm her mother? It seemed that all the answers rested on finding the woman who had given her life.

"So what exactly do you think we're looking for?" She half turned in her chair to direct the question to Derek.

"Like you said, anything from the time you were born through toddlerhood. That's our best window, considering the dates on your birth certificate." He didn't look up from his papers.

Hannah scrolled through articles, pausing to skim the most promising ones, but came up empty for the first several months after her birth. Perhaps it was a ridiculous quest. Was it foolish even to think that whatever had put her in danger as a baby would have made the news? It could have been a secret endeavor at the time, or something that the head honchos at the newspaper didn't think was worthy of paper and ink. Derek had indicated that her birth father was part of an organized crime family, and certainly a connection with the mob could prove deadly, both then and now. Perhaps she should focus on headlines that concerned the Mafia, except those were few and far between.

As she scanned through headlines from nine months after her birth, one about an organized crime arrest caught her attention. She pulled up the entire article on the screen and was immediately assaulted by a photo of a woman who was almost the exact image of herself, holding a child with a doll just like the one that had been her childhood favorite. Was this her mother? "Derek." A hoarse whisper was all she could muster.

He instantly appeared at her side, one hand on the back of her chair and the other on the table as he leaned in to look closely at the photo. His strong jaw was just inches away, and she struggled to remove her stare from the photo on the computer screen and focus on something else, like Derek's solid, reassuring presence. But she couldn't do it.

"I think that's my mother."

"Looks like it. Then that's you she's holding. What does the article say?"

"I don't know. I haven't read it yet." She shook her head to force her eyes away from the image, but she couldn't. She started to skim the story.

When she tried to read it, though, the words swam on the screen. She squeezed her eyes shut, and a tear pushed out. "Can you tell me what it says, please?"

"Of course." Derek laid a comforting hand on her shoulder then returned it to the back of the chair.

For that brief moment when she'd felt his touch, peace and calm had enveloped her. Now the void overwhelmed her. She leaned back, seeking his hand again, and closed her eyes.

"It's about the arrest of a Mafia enforcer. Police happened upon what looked like a murder scene but there was no body." He paused as he read further. "It wasn't far outside Chicago. A vehicle crashed down an embankment. The authorities suspected foul play since they found blood and hair in the car. DNA was matched to a woman."

"What was her name?" *Was it Susan?*

"No name was released. The police were holding the suspect, a white male."

"Is there a photo of him?"

"No."

She felt Derek move his hand from the back of her chair and lean toward the mouse as she watched lights flicker and flash across the insides of her eyelids.

"There's just one more article, a short piece toward the bottom of the page that was published a couple of days later."

"And?" She fluttered her eyes open only to see the light from the screen shining on her, and then closed them again.

"The suspect was released due to lack of evidence. Apparently, no body had been found. No body means they can't prove murder." He paused again. When he spoke, his voice was hesitant. "Hannah, there's a picture."

She popped her eyes open. A man stared back at her. His sullen expression didn't look anything like the image she saw in the mirror every morning. His hair was the same dark brown, but that was all the similarity she could see. It didn't seem likely that he was her father. But if the danger was enough that her mother felt forced to give her up for adoption, then wasn't it logical that this man was her father?

"Sean O'Shea? That's his name?" She squinted at the words under the photo.

"Yeah, that's the name the FBI has on record. But he's not the man who shot at us at your parents' house."

"What does that mean?"

"Most likely, Sean O'Shea is the mastermind behind all this, and the thug who's been after us is working with him or for him."

"We need to keep looking. Keep digging."

The woman who looked like her, who had disappeared, was unknown to her. How should she feel about it all? Of course she was sad that perhaps the woman had died. The loss of human life should always carry some weight of sorrow. But she didn't know her. The woman was probably her birth mother, and the man was supposed to be her birth father, but she didn't know beyond a reasonable doubt. There was no relationship with either of them for the possibility of their deaths to feel like a true personal loss to her. That thought alone deepened the sadness.

"So this is why your biological father kept looking for your birth mother." Derek pulled up a chair and sat next to her. "From what is stated in this article, it isn't clear that she died. Her body was never found. It looks like a classic maneuver to make everyone think she's dead when she really just escaped."

Hannah's heart pounded as she gripped the chair's armrests. "You said earlier that she's alive and my birth father had found her."

"Yes. But a lot could have happened since we acquired that information. Things that would never make the news and that would take us time to discover."

"Right. But what about the adoption registry? She could have registered in that online database, putting her information out there for her daughter—for me—to find her someday." Was it possible that it would be that easy?

"That's doubtful. I know you want information, but think about it from a lawyer's perspective. Not as her probable daughter.

Wouldn't registering in a public forum like that expose her identity and possible location to whomever she was escaping?"

"Couldn't I register, then? She could see it and contact me through private channels."

"Hannah." He took her hand, the lines around his eyes creased with empathy and concern. "Remember the letter from your birth mother? She instructed you not to search for her. And now someone is after you. You would be exposing yourself as well. We've done what we can here, and it's been helpful. But you can't open yourself up to all those creeps who lurk online."

Shoulders slumped, she pulled her hand out from underneath Derek's and stood. It was time to go. She wasn't sure where, but she couldn't find any more information now.

They replaced their chairs and made their way back through the empty basement toward the stairs. The library would be closing soon, and it seemed that most of the patrons had gone.

As they passed the last of the stacks, a man stepped out of the shadows. The barrel of his gun pressed against Hannah's ribs. She gasped, her body tensing, and she fisted her hands at her sides. Derek turned toward him, his face hardened, as if he was in attack mode.

"Don't even," the man growled near her ear and jabbed his gun deeper into her side. "Reach for your weapon and she's dead." She arched toward Derek, wincing from the pain and pressure, but the man grabbed her opposite arm and held her close. Derek's face contorted with his fury at being ambushed, but she couldn't even manage a whisper to him. "I'm going to take you both out of here nice and quiet. I have my orders, but this isn't the place for it. Head for the stairs, and walk out like all is normal."

Derek slowly turned toward the steps, his back almost completely toward her. She couldn't see his face or read his expressions, so there was no hope of picking up on any indicators of what he had planned. Surely, he had something in mind. He would get them out of this...or die trying.

A couple of feet from the bottom of the stairs, they passed a reading table with a large stack of books on it that hadn't been shelved yet. One step past the books, Derek twisted his upper body and jerked his elbow out toward the books. He hit them off the table with the back of his arm. The books flew off the desk and landed at the feet of Hannah and the gunman, who held her in a vise grip.

The man stumbled on the books and let loose a few choice words at Derek. He lost his hold on Hannah as the gun swung away from her in his effort to keep his balance. She jerked free and lunged toward a thick dictionary on a nearby stand. Grasping it firmly, she swung back around toward the assailant. The dictionary connected with his head. A crack resounded throughout the basement as the man crumpled to the floor.

She dropped the dictionary on the table as Derek grabbed her hand and pulled her away from the man now lying still on the floor. She heaved out a breath and her stomach churned, but she managed to stay upright.

Derek grabbed the man's gun and placed it on the table, keeping his own SIG trained on the attacker, then stepped in front of Hannah in a protective stance. As soon as she stilled behind him, he kneeled beside the man and pressed his first and second fingers to the man's throat. Hannah's attacker was still alive with a strong heartbeat, but he seemed to be out cold.

He quickly dialed Square and reported

the incident. With instructions to hold the man until local law enforcement arrived, he quickly surveyed the immediate area of the basement for something with which to tie up the man.

But there was nothing. And his handcuffs had remained on the goon that had attacked them at the McClarnons'. At least the librarians and other patrons weren't in danger. Considering the modus operandi of the thugs so far, Derek surmised that this man wouldn't want to do anything to draw the attention of law enforcement to himself. Covert attacks were the method. That meant that Derek needed to heighten his alert. He would not fail in his first assignment. He would protect Hannah to the best of his ability, hopefully receive a pat on the back from his supervising agent and move on to the next assignment.

The air conditioning kicked on and blew wisps of Hannah's hair across her face as he stood and turned back to her. He itched to tuck it behind her ears, to gently brush the back of his hand against her cheek. Her resiliency and quick thinking surprised him. He had completed training at the FBI academy to improve his response time, but she was going on instinct. Her maneuver had been well-executed and definitely successful.

He glanced at the heavy dictionary on the table. It appeared to be undamaged, despite its use as a bludgeon. Words had power. Too many times, words failed him, and he felt like he was going to choke just trying to communicate what was in his mind. But if he could wield a dictionary that well to verbalize, well, things might be different between him and Hannah. If he could have been well-spoken and confident with her father back in high school, perhaps life would have taken a different course.

Derek sighed. It wouldn't do to dwell on regret now. Nothing would change the past, and the future seemed to be set as well. His position with the FBI was secure. It would be lonely, a job on the go, devoid of romantic relationships. But it was the least he could do for his parents. To honor both their lives and their deaths.

"You did well, Hannah." His voice sounded stiff and formal to his ears, but that seemed the best way to handle a woman whose very presence threatened to distract him from his work. "I can't leave him—" he nodded toward the man still lying motionless on the floor "—and I don't want to send you upstairs alone. But the library staff needs to know the police are coming. Do you have a phone number for your librarian friend?"

"I can get one." She worked her phone and was soon informing Tallulah of the events that had unfolded in the lower level. As she talked, Derek kept his hand on her elbow to help her stay calm and reassured of their safety. If the photos in the newspaper on the microfilm had been what they seemed, and there was no reason to doubt their authenticity, Hannah's birth father was most definitely dangerous. Most likely, he was even the one who made her birth mother feel so unsafe she had to put her little girl up for adoption. Was he the one behind these attacks?

That twist of maliciousness in the man's expression was the same brand of evil that haunted his memories. Derek rubbed his forehead as if that could dispel the reminder of his parents and the horrific images that seemed always to hover at the edge of his consciousness. No matter what happened next, he would keep Hannah safe from her own father, a man who didn't deserve that label.

"Derek?" Hannah nudged him to get his attention. "I told Tallulah that she'll be safe.

Right? The police are on their way." She held her phone up and indicated that it was on speaker.

He pictured the librarian's kind face as Hannah's soft voice wrapped around him. "Yes. I hear the sirens."

"I do as well." Tallulah's voice came through the phone loud and clear. "My prayers for your safety and well-being go with you. Remember the promise in Psalm 121. 'The Lord shall preserve you from all evil; He shall preserve your soul. The Lord shall preserve your going out and your coming in from this time forth, and even forevermore.' May it be as the Lord has promised."

"Thank you." Derek appreciated the prayer, but he hadn't closed his eyes. He was sure the Lord understood his need to keep a close watch on the man on the floor.

"Amen," Hannah whispered.

He checked the time on her phone as she ended the call. The library would be closing in a few minutes and, most likely, nearly all the patrons would be gone. He exhaled his first breath of relief since he'd protected Hannah at the Callahans' office building earlier. A moan escaped from the thug lying on the floor. Derek glanced at Hannah, who was looking nervously back at her attacker.

"IMPD!" The shout preceded the police officers down the stairs, and soon the gunman was handcuffed.

Derek holstered his SIG and handed over the man's weapon, then spent the next several minutes briefing the officers. As soon as the goon regained consciousness, the officers placed him under arrest and hauled him up the stairs. Derek steered Hannah, with her armful of books and her tote, toward the elevator back to the parking garage. Perhaps now they could find rest and a place to lie low until the danger was over.

Before he allowed Hannah into the elevator, he stepped one foot in and checked the ceiling tiles. With no sign of tampering, he ushered her in. In the couple of minutes it would take to get to the garage, he called his supervising special agent to let him know the attacker was in custody.

His supervisor's voice filled his ear. "Good work. There are officers on the street around the parking garage to stop anyone suspicious who may be leaving. You've seen two different men already. No telling how many more there might be, so be careful."

"If it's the same vehicle that was tailing us before, it's a dark-colored truck with a star-shaped police organization sticker on the front windshield. We're now in a blue Corolla."

With one more instruction from his supervisor to keep in touch and maintain a low profile, Derek reholstered his cell.

The elevator doors opened and Derek put a protective arm across Hannah as he peered out into the garage. All seemed still, but he laid a hand on his SIG Sauer just in case.

As they exited the elevator, Hannah shuddered. "I know we got the guy, but I always have the willies in a parking lot after dark. Parking garages are even worse." She huddled closer to Derek.

Florescent lights flickered overhead, but it wasn't enough for safety. The red and blue of law enforcement vehicles flashed dimly up the exit ramp.

As they headed toward the Corolla, Derek scanned the parking garage. A few cars were still there, probably belonging to library employees. All seemed well, until Hannah wobbled in her footing and leaned heavily into his side.

Memories of their Friday nights here assailed him. One night in particular permeated his mind, the Friday right before Mr. McClarnon had ordered him to end the relationship.

"What is it?" Hannah asked, her arm tense against his, as if she feared more trouble.

"What do you mean?"

"You shivered. Did you see something? Is someone here?"

He had shivered? That was the power of memories, Derek supposed. "Do you remember the very last time we were here together? In this parking garage?"

In the flickering lights, he could see a grin creep across her lips. "Yes. We parked over there." She nodded to a far corner, and the grin disappeared. "It was dark like this, and you were holding my hand."

"We took our time because we knew we had to part ways and go home."

"And when we got to the car, you took my books in one arm, put the other arm around me..."

"Our one and only stolen kiss." Even then, ten years later, Derek remembered the feel of her in his arms, her soft lips on his. Would it—could it—happen again?

His shoe hit a pebble and he kicked it across a few parking spaces. Reality slapped him on the back. A relationship with Hannah, a true and lasting marriage with a woman who shared his goals and dreams, would never work. Her father had made it clear how he felt about Derek, and there was nothing to indicate that he had changed his mind. He would not come between Hannah and her parents. She needed them now more than ever. Plus, he was at the very beginning of a career with the FBI and recalled the promise he'd made to himself after his parents were killed. There was no room for a wife and family with so much travel and trouble around every turn. And he wouldn't abandon them, like he had been abandoned.

Whether it was on purpose or simply an accidental wobble, it didn't matter. Hannah stepped away from him as they approached the vehicle, a quiet reminder that she wasn't in the market for a relationship, either. Not with him. Not with anybody.

But when she approached the car, she didn't walk around to the passenger side. Instead, she placed her stack of hardback books on the roof and then turned to face him. She looked at him with an expression he couldn't quite fathom, a mixture, it seemed, of contemplation and longing and grief.

He stepped close, the keys in his hand. He would have to lean around her to unlock the door. In the midst of the car fumes of the garage, he inhaled her scent—a light floral aroma that tingled his senses. He had to stay on alert. There could be danger lurking in the darkness of the garage. He stepped toward her, his arm reaching around her waist, beginning to draw her away from the door handle.

The click-clack of steps drew his attention away from Hannah, and a gravelly voice assailed him. "Well, isn't this romantic."

Hannah stiffened in his hold, and he spun around. Shadows concealed the speaker's facial features, but Derek couldn't miss the glint of the gun that was pointed at both of them. Was this a partner of the guy they had knocked unconscious in the library? Had he been waiting for them?

Maybe FBI agents weren't supposed to ever be scared, but a chill stair-stepped up Derek's spine at the malicious voice and the deadly weapon pointed at them.

SIX

Hannah dug her fingers into Derek's arm, glad he was willing to hide her behind him yet desperate that he not be hurt. Where did these guys keep coming from? Whoever was behind these attacks, he seemed to have an army of minions covering Hannah and Derek wherever they went. Just when they thought they were safe, another gunman appeared.

Tears sprang to her eyes. She was ready to call it quits, to give them whatever they wanted, to give up to them. The man had gotten the drop on them, and Derek hadn't even had time to grab his weapon in defense. It had been all her fault, as she'd been distracted by the presence of a handsome man. The dim light in the parking garage glinted off the man's gun, and Hannah squinted in the reflection as prisms of light floated through her teary vision.

She shifted her view to Derek's back to break the glare on her eyes. He had his hands at his sides, unable to move without alerting their assailant. What was the plan now? Could she figure out how to get them away before the man forced her out from behind Derek? She loosened her grip on Derek's arm, but that didn't release any of the tension in his bicep. Her other hand was behind him, and their attacker hadn't insisted yet that she come forward.

Inch by inch, she reached behind her to the car door. Hope shot through her when she realized she could just reach the handle and get her fingers under it to lift up. She pressed her other fingers into Derek's arm as if she was about to pull him around, then sent a prayer heavenward that he would understand her signal.

Barely breathing, she urged herself to go for it, then jerked her hand from Derek's arm in the same way she'd jerked on the door handle. Derek must have understood her signal, for at her motion, he punched the gun out of the startled man's hand. It skittered across the parking garage floor.

The man grabbed at the car door, the tips of his fingers on the top edge in an effort to hold it open. She slammed the door shut with all of her strength. The man cried out and grasped his wrist. She opened the door again, and he stumbled back, holding his wrist with his other hand and glaring at his fingers.

Behind her, Derek urged her into the vehicle. Hannah crawled across to the passenger seat, pulling her feet up to allow space for Derek to jump into the driver's seat. Their attacker still held his wrist, looking from them to his gun, seemingly uncertain as to what his next move should be. It didn't take long for him to decide, and he quickly stumbled to retrieve his weapon.

Derek glanced at her as she continued to unfold herself from her crawling position into the passenger seat. "You good?"

"Yes. Go! Go!"

He threw the car into Drive and stepped on the accelerator. As the tires squealed against the pavement and caught some traction, Hannah turned to see their attacker gain his footing and dash to within a few feet of the car. He was pointing his gun at Derek.

But as the car took off, the books Hannah had left on the roof of the car flew off. One hardback book smacked the man in his chest. The other catapulted into his head. It bounced off, leaving a trail of red oozing down his forehead. The impact forced him to step back just as he squeezed the trigger, his arms waving to keep his balance. The shot arced toward the ceiling. Bits of cement rained down on the roof of the car.

Derek turned sharply, and Hannah grabbed the door handle to stay upright. The Corolla zipped around the garage toward the exit. Another shot rang out and hit a cement pillar as the car screeched behind it.

Ducking down, Hannah peered through the space between the top of the seat and the headrest. She jabbed the moisture from her cheeks and forced herself to breathe. They were safe. For now.

Before she could relax, a third thug emerged from the elevator and joined the second. She tapped Derek's arm. "Another one," she whispered and nodded behind them. "Was he in the library, too?"

He looked in the rearview mirror, a grim set to his mouth. "Sit down. Hold tight."

She quickly fastened her seat belt and fisted the hem of her shirt to dry her palms.

An engine revved behind them. Tires squealed on the cement as they raced for the exit ramp. Derek hit it as fast as seemed safe, but the vehicle felt airborne for a moment before they crashed back to the ground.

The Corolla sped out of the parking garage, past a couple of sheriff's vehicles and a van. Derek cranked the wheel and turned a hard left onto the street. The thugs shot out a few moments later. The sheriff's vehicles immediately flipped on their sirens and apprehended them a couple of blocks down the road. As Hannah peeked around the front seat, the thugs were removed from their truck and put in the back of the sheriff's van.

Was it over now? The thumping of her heart told her it wasn't yet. She raked a hand through her hair and released a quavering breath. "What do you think?" Perhaps Derek would have an encouraging word.

"Not clear yet." He changed lanes abruptly, shifting his focus from the front windshield to the rearview mirror and then to the side mirror. "Close, though." He rolled through a stop on Meridian Street, checking both ways before focusing on the road ahead again.

A sudden bump rocked her forward in tandem with Derek. "What was that?" She spun around to see the sheriff's van backing off before the engine revved and the vehicle slammed forward again.

"That's not the deputy at the wheel." Determination tinged with irritation laced his words.

Hannah touched her hand to her forehead. It came away damp with perspiration. "What happened to the sheriff's deputies? I hope they're all right." She bit the side of her lip. "I hope we're okay."

Derek retrieved his phone. "I'll call the sheriff. See if they're okay and find out what's going on."

"What should I do? I need to do something."

"Pray."

Derek spoke briefly into the phone, weaving through downtown traffic with one hand on the wheel. He hung up and placed the phone on the console in between the seats without taking his eyes off the road. "They're fine."

Hannah sighed with relief. "What happened?"

"They're not sure. Got out of the zip ties somehow." He turned a fast right onto Monument Circle. "They took over the van so quickly they must have figured we weren't too far away yet."

"At least there's isn't much going on downtown tonight." Hannah peeked back again and found the sheriff's van right behind them. Both vehicles had slowed so as not to endanger the few pedestrians that dotted the downtown sidewalks. "Would they try anything in front of these people?"

"I doubt it. They'd leave evidence and probably get caught again." Even as he finished his sentence, sirens pierced the air.

Three quarters of the way around the circle, the theater stood tall. What she wouldn't give to be at the symphony right now instead of in this high-speed car chase. Soothing music instead of sirens. Red velvet seats instead of the Corolla's vinyl. Derek in a dark blue suit and jaunty tie instead of…

Whoa. Her thoughts were racing away as far as the bad guys. She gripped the seat belt and pulled it away from her neck. She was straining forward so much that it was probably pressing a red mark into her neck.

With the sheriff's van close behind, Derek turned right onto Market Street. A block later, he jerked the car south onto Pennsylvania.

"Where are we going?" Her voice sounded much calmer than she felt. But her stomach roiled at the sudden turns, and a bitterness rose at the back of her throat.

"Not sure. But I don't want to get them on a straightaway, where they can gain speed."

He turned again, and a three-story mall came into view. Pedestrian traffic increased in this part of downtown, and Derek slowed the car. The aroma of a pretzel shop wafted into the vehicle, and Hannah glanced toward it, half of a prayer on her lips.

A second later, she returned her gaze to the road. A young couple holding hands had stepped out into the street, right into their lane.

"Derek! Look out!"

At Hannah's scream, Derek tore his attention from the rearview mirror. Two people stood directly in the path of the Corolla. He hit the horn, touched the brakes and swerved into the next lane with barely a glance to his blind spot. *Lord, help!*

The car in his blind spot honked, but the scream of tires assured him that the other guy got out of the way. The couple jumped back, the woman clapping her hand to her mouth in fright. Derek barreled through, but the sheriff's van had lost a little distance.

Hannah gripped the armrest and swiveled to look back. "They're all right. They look dazed, but they're okay." She swung back to the front. "Why don't they just rear-end us? Take us somehow?"

Derek tapped the brakes then hit his signal and jumped into another lane. "They're in a sheriff's vehicle, but they're not in uniform. It'd be safer not to exit and call attention to themselves."

"We can't continue like this all night. What do we do? Drive until someone runs out of gas?"

"Law enforcement is on the way. They'll get them." They better. He was running out of options, despite the rigorous training he'd had on the precision course at the academy.

Should he get them to the federal building a couple of blocks away, where they could run inside and let their security handle it? There was always someone on duty, no matter the hour. But would the thugs driving the van follow them inside or just shoot Derek and Hannah as they ran? The doors probably wouldn't be open anyway, and he didn't want to crash through the gate and into the interior parking area. And did he really want to complicate the situation with yet another division of the law-enforcement agency involved?

There was another option, though. Why not ditch the Corolla?

He merged into the traffic on Washington Street. The mall parking garage beckoned on the left side, but he drove on. He definitely did not want another underground parking garage. Restaurants lined the other side of the street, their outdoor lights twinkling as patrons smiled at one another over iced tea or lemonade. Maybe when this was over, he'd bring Hannah downtown for an evening out, a stroll around the circle, perhaps a horse-and-carriage ride. Out where everyone could see them. No hiding, like in high school.

He shook his head to clear it of the image of Hannah in evening attire, a lightweight sweater draped over her slender shoulders. That visual wouldn't help them at all right now. It would, in fact, cause only more problems. He needed to get his head in the game and get them both safe.

He pulled deep into the traffic, glancing in the rearview mirror to see two angry faces scowling at him, but not so closely that he could distinguish any features. He maneuvered through the lanes until the faces disappeared, putting a tall Coca-Cola delivery truck between the Corolla and the thugs in the sheriff's van. An empty city bus pulled up in the left lane as all lanes stopped at a red light.

"Get your bag, and let's go. Chinese fire drill."

She spun toward him, her hand on her purse, a look of confusion and skepticism etched on her beautiful face. "What? Leave the safety of the car?"

"Yes, but we're not switching drivers. We're abandoning the vehicle. Follow me."

He popped open his door and, leaning low, peered out.

No sheriff's van in sight. He didn't dare to hope that meant they were safe, but it would buy them a little bit of time.

He motioned to Hannah to follow, and she scooted across his seat, keeping her head below the headrests. Clasping her hand in his, he stepped up to the city bus and rapped on the door. The bus driver was staring straight into the traffic and flailed in his seat when Derek knocked. Eyes wide, he shook his head *no* and gripped the bus's steering wheel. Derek retrieved his badge from his belt and flashed it at the driver. The man wouldn't have any choice now.

The door lurched open, and Derek whispered a thank-you to the driver. He pushed

Hannah in first. "Stay low. Head down the center aisle and lie down."

She got onto her hands and knees and crawled several feet down the aisle. Derek followed, keeping his voice low to instruct the driver. "You off duty now?"

"Yep," the driver said softly. "Heading home. Problem?"

"Just act normal and continue your route."

He raised up enough to peer out the windows. The light hadn't changed yet, and the thugs in the sheriff's van were stuck two cars back.

"FBI, sir. Please just sit as you normally would. Look forward, not down at us on the floor, and everything will be fine."

He lowered himself back to the grimy floor, facing the driver and far enough forward that he could peek out the long windows in the door. What was Hannah's impression of her surroundings now? Gum wrappers, some with bits of chewed gum clinging to them, were scattered around, along with paper receipts, rocks and debris off of shoes, half-eaten French fries. It was gross and disgusting and the only escape he could think of.

Whatever he'd thought of Hannah before, and it had been a considerable impression, it was just elevated. She hadn't protested or run. The girl who had grown up in luxury and opulence had followed his plan without debate and now was lying on the gritty floor of a city bus. Add *resilient* to her long list of positive characteristics.

Derek cleared his throat and tapped the driver's knee to get his attention. "Don't look down at me, but I need to know what's going on out there without revealing my position. Nod if you understand."

The guy nodded slightly. He would do well.

"Do you see a sheriff's van?"

The driver leaned forward in his seat to peer out the side-view mirror as he pushed on the accelerator and the bus lurched forward. The light must have changed. "Yes. Behind us and to the right a couple of cars. It's moving forward now, around a car in the middle of the road."

"Do you see two men in it?"

"One."

"One?" Hannah's panicked whisper reached his ears. "Where'd the other one go?"

Derek felt her hand on his ankle, as she sought reassurance. "Safety is our concern. Right now, we're good. Just stay low." It may be the grimy floor of a city bus, but at least she was with him, and he could be assured that she was well.

He rolled to his side and retrieved his cell. A hushed conversation with his supervisor lasted less than a minute. It ended with the instruction to continue to stay low.

Derek closed his eyes briefly. He had to make a plan. The Corolla was gone, so they had no transportation. He had no idea where the bus terminal was, but he figured he had the authority to commandeer the vehicle. And when providing protective custody, keeping the woman as far away as possible from the bad guys was always the best game plan.

"Driver, we need to get to the airport. Since you're done with your route, let's head straight there." He had a buddy with the airport police, and there were plenty of rental car agencies there as well.

"Uh—" the driver glanced down at him then quickly returned his attention to the road "—that's not on my way."

What was up with this guy? Didn't the FBI badge mean anything, or did Derek need to work on his authoritative command? "I understand your eagerness to get home, but we're in a bit of a jam here. Make an exception."

He peered out the door window again to

find the sheriff's van pulled up alongside the bus. He jerked back behind the seats, digging his elbow right into a gooey piece of gum on the floor. Derek inched forward to dare another peek through the window. The thug from the library sat in the driver's seat, a scowl on his face as his gaze swept the bus. A tremor of panic swept through Derek.

SEVEN

One more flash of the badge had convinced the bus driver to head to the airport straight away. Their position had been undetected, and a couple of miles out of downtown, Derek had motioned Hannah up into a seat. He still wasn't sure what their overnight plan would be, but as they pulled away from the city lights, he could see the stars twinkling in the cool, clear night.

At least they would be a long, long way from Heartwood Hill, on the other side of Indianapolis. Hopefully away from anywhere those jerks might think to look for Hannah. At Derek's instruction, the bus driver pulled up to the passenger drop-off at the airport. He said thanks to the driver as he dragged his shoe across the pavement in a vain effort to get the gum loose.

As they descended the steps, he held Hannah's elbow. "Just smile and look straight ahead."

She plastered on a grin, but he could still see the worry in the lines around her eyes. "What are we doing here?"

"A friend of mine is with the airport police. We were on the force in Heartwood Hill together. And we can rent another vehicle."

With a thorough look around, he led her through the automatic doors and into the main terminal. A handful of people sat in a waiting area, and one man watched the arrival and departure boards. Even though Indianapolis was considered a major metropolitan airport, it turned fairly quiet later in the evening. Only so many flights could come and go based on customer capacity.

They walked calmly and approached the escalator down to the baggage claim. At the bottom, he stopped to pretend to look at a large map on a lit board. If anyone was tailing them, they wouldn't be able to hide in such a sparse crowd. Five minutes later, Derek was convinced they had not been followed.

"We're almost there. Ready to stop and take a break?"

She slung her purse over her shoulder to

carry it cross-body style and sighed. "I'm ready to eat something and lie down for the night. Is that possible?"

He wouldn't promise anything he couldn't follow through on, but he wanted to reassure her. "I think so, but let me make a call first."

He quickly dialed his friend from his days on the force, sending up a quick prayer that he would be on duty. Three rings later, his prayer was answered, and Tyler had offered a place to crash for the night. He had also offered to send a car for them, but Derek thought it might be best if they approached under cover of darkness rather than in a marked police vehicle.

Hannah had leaned against the sign and closed her eyes.

He put a hand on her shoulder, and she opened one eye at him.

"We're good."

She adopted a weary smile, and his heart flopped as he took her hand. He couldn't help holding her hand as they walked. It felt so natural. And yet, he really shouldn't. Once she was safe and the assignment was over, he would move on, and she would return to law school. There was no point in either of them having unrealistic expectations or hopes. Leading Hannah out the automatic doors and onto the sidewalk outside baggage claim, Derek stepped into the landscaping. He skirted the building, down toward the runways around the back of the large structure. Only moonlight guided them, as well as whatever florescent glow reached that far from passenger pickup and the parking areas in the distance. Dew had begun to gather on the grass, and Hannah slipped into his arms as they descended. He quickly righted her and set her aside despite the thumping of his heart.

As they approached the bottom and secure pavement again, a rustling in the bushes spooked her. She leaped toward Derek and grabbed onto his shirt sleeve as a raccoon waddled from the foliage. They stood for a moment, watching the masked bandit make his way across the mulch. A memory surfaced from high school, a time in their secluded part of the library when she had asked for help understanding a complicated math concept. He had scooted his chair closer to hers and laid his arm on the back of her chair. But before they were done with the tutorial, his arm had completely enclosed her shoulders. Derek hadn't moved his arm for the rest of the study session, despite the fact that it had gone tingly with sleep after just thirty minutes.

Now, ten years later, he was prepared to protect her from all sorts of scary things.

But there was only one sort of scary thing he was responsible for now, and those guys seemed lost at the moment.

Around the corner, the runways stretched in front of them. To the side, a large glowing sign—Indianapolis Airport Police Department—beckoned them. The entrance was an out-of-the-way place with what looked like virtually no foot or vehicular traffic this time of night, but Derek hoped and prayed that safety and rest and refreshment were within reach.

Tyler opened the door as they approached. When Derek walked through behind Hannah, Tyler slapped him on the shoulder, a gesture of comfort and reassurance that he hadn't realized he needed. There had been no doubt in his mind months ago at the beginning of his training at the FBI academy that this was what he had wanted. Ever since his parents' murders, he had been bound and determined to join the FBI. But now that he had reached his goal, it would take some adjustment. And his reunion with his high school sweetheart had added to the stress of a first assignment.

Along with the slap on the back from Tyler came raised eyebrows and a nod toward Hannah. Derek shook his head. No, they were not a couple, although he increasingly wanted them to be.

Once they were inside, Tyler pulled the door closed and a lock clicked inside. "We're hidden away on the back side of the terminal, and it gets pretty quiet. But after hours, no one gets in without their security pass." He pulled an ID card out of his pocket to show them how it electronically unlocked the door. "Not many come and go through the night, but you'll be safe here."

A lingering odor of stale coffee assaulted him upon entry. Without passing anyone on the way, Tyler escorted them to the break room, which had fluorescent lights, a couple of black leather tufted sofas and a kitchenette flanked by a full garbage can. He was appreciative of Tyler's offer and knew that cleanup would happen whenever it could, around a police officer's busy shift.

Tyler gestured toward a couple of vending machines, one that dispensed plastic bottles of pop and another that had chips and cookies and candy bars. "We don't have much, but make yourself at home. You can get a snack from the machines, and we have bottles of water in the refrigerator. You can make some coffee, but I'm guessing you'd rather catch some sleep. Settle in on the sofas. We have a couple of blankets in the storage cabinet." At Hannah's inquisitive look, he explained, "Sometimes officers take a quick nap in between shifts. It saves time from going home."

Derek shook his hand. "Thanks. I don't know how I can repay you."

"No need. Whatever your case, I've never known any perps to walk right into a police station. During the day, officers might be in and out for break time or to get some paperwork done. But in the middle of the night, you may not see anyone. If you do, they'll be quiet."

"Thanks again."

"We'll catch up another time, pal, all right? Right now, I'm getting home, and you need some rest." Tyler smiled at Hannah and left them alone.

Derek ambled to the vending machine and took his time selecting a few items for both of them. They were safe, it was quiet and Hannah's floral scent was beginning to overpower the stale feel of the room. He breathed deeply, savoring the moment, uncertain when there might be another pause in the chase.

He turned to find that she had set the table as best she could. Paper plates sat in front of chairs across from each other. Paper napkins were set to the left. A bottle of water finished the place setting at the upper right. She would probably have placed a vase of fresh flowers in the middle if she could have found some, and he admired her all the more for her ability to turn even the most dire of circumstances into something worth relishing.

He held out his findings to her. "Do you want the plain potato chips or the ones with sour cream and chives?" He offered what felt like a weak grin, but there wasn't anything more he could do.

"Whichever you don't want."

"I don't care. You choose."

"You choose first. I'll take whatever's left." A smile played around her lips.

"Come on. This is an on-the-job meal for me. I was warned at the academy that there would be plenty of drive-thrus and vending machines in my future career. But you've sacrificed a lot to be here."

"Like what? A microwaved meal?"

"Like steak and lobster and fresh home-made bread served to you on fine china." He figured she lived in the family mansion, and this was a long way from that opulent life-style. Their differences, and the reason they could never be together, could not be more obvious than right there in the police-station break room.

"No one serves me in my apartment. It's me and my new best friend, the microwave."

"Really? Hannah McClarnon eats micro-wave meals?" He regretted it as soon as he said it.

Hurt filled her soft, brown eyes.

How could he say such a thing to her? Where was his faith? Had the frustration of his first assignment been too much? He placed both bags of chips on her paper plate. "I'm sorry. Here. You take them both. I'm not hungry anyway."

She selected one and opened it, dumping the chips on her plate. Whether or not it was her first choice he didn't know, but it didn't seem to matter now. She put a chip in her mouth and chewed slowly, a tear slipping down her cheek.

He grasped one of her hands. "I'm sorry, Hannah. I just...I know I'm not good enough for you. Your father made that clear. And I guess it just slipped out. Please forgive me."

She nodded, and he prayed that was her assent.

"So you're really serious about this legal career, huh? Your own apartment?"

"Definitely, despite what my parents want."

"Being a little rebellious?" He forced a smile to ease the moment. Hannah was so gentle and devoted to her family that he couldn't imagine her as an all-out rebel.

"This is as much rebellion as I can muster. I just feel really strongly that this is God's will for me. That I can do more good with a law degree than I can attending country-club receptions and directing the gardener where to plant the zinnias."

"Your parents can't see that?" he asked softly.

"If they do, they don't show it. It would be nice to get a word of encouragement every now and then, but for the moment, it's enough to know that I'm in God's will."

He released her hand reluctantly and twisted the cap on his water bottle. "They'll come around eventually. It's obvious how much they love and admire you. Once they see what a terrific lawyer you become, it'll be fine."

She ran a hand through her hair, then stood and threw away her plate. "I'm tired of thinking about it all. I need to lie down."

With her face turned toward the back of the sofa, Hannah listened to Derek's whispers. It seemed that he was praying, but she couldn't make out the words. She trusted Derek, even if he didn't seem to trust himself.

She had always had faith in him, but apparently others had not. That comment about her father was mystifying. Had something happened or someone said something that she didn't know about? She had told Derek she didn't want to think about it all, but she couldn't shut down her mind.

Hannah shifted to face him, pulling the blanket around with her and smoothing it. He sat on the opposite sofa, his head bowed but his eyes open. Always alert. Always vigilant.

Footsteps sounded outside the door, and a bumping came from down the hall. Voices rose and fell. All normal noises from a police station at night, she assumed. The door to the break room swung open, and a uniformed police officer entered. He nodded at Derek, grabbed a bottle of water from the refrigerator and left.

"I can't sleep."

He ran a hand through his hair then scrubbed it against his cheek. "You should try to rest. I hope this all ends soon, but if it doesn't, you should sleep now."

"What about you? You need rest, too."

"Nope. FBI agents don't sleep. Didn't you know?" He offered a smile, but even in the faint glow of the fluorescent lights, she could see how weary he was.

"I keep thinking that this is just not the day I thought it was going to be. All I wanted to do was go to work, get some great experience that might lead to a permanent position after law school, then go home and read a novel." She swiped hair off her forehead. "And now? Now, I've been shot at—how many times? Not exactly a normal occurrence in an average citizen's life. I'm glad we have a place to rest, but a couch at the airport police station? I'm not complaining, but I never would have predicted this when I woke up this morning."

"I'm sure it's been a little confusing for you, especially with the news I had to bring to you."

"So this is going to be your life now, as an FBI agent? Always on the run?"

"I can't say I know for sure, since I'm a newbie. Some parts of the job will probably be boring, but there's also sure to be more of this."

"More girls that need your protection?" Where did that come from? He had been hers at one point in time, but not anymore. Before today, she hadn't heard from him in years. Now, he returned with a job to do, but that didn't mean he was here to see her. Not for personal reasons, at least, despite how much she was beginning to want it to be so. Yet, a knot had formed in her stomach at the thought of him with someone else. She pressed a hand to her middle as if that would assuage the onslaught. "I'm sorry. That was uncalled for."

Mixed emotions crossed his handsome face. Frustration? Or was there a hint of pleasure in her possessiveness there as well?

Maybe she should come right out and ask. Honesty was the best policy and all that. A lump clogged her throat. The question that was at the forefront of her mind seemed riskier somehow than running from the bad guys with guns. "I've just been wondering. Not all this time, of course. But since you reappeared this afternoon. What ever happened with us? One day things were great, and we were planning which college we could attend together. The next day, you wanted nothing to do with me."

She swallowed hard. "The last time I saw you was at graduation. I spotted your cap a couple of rows over, but you never turned to make eye contact. I guess we both suspected from the beginning that our relationship couldn't work. That's why we kept it secret. But then, by the end, I thought we were thinking of ways to make a go of it. What did I do?"

She'd pushed those thoughts of rejection out of her mind for years, focusing first on college and then law school, rejecting the advances of any other man. It couldn't have been her, could it have been? Did guys just decide one day that they were done with a relationship and leave? Hannah hadn't thought that Derek was one of those types.

He cleared his throat and adopted a look of chagrin, taking a long look at the floor before he finally met her gaze. "There's probably something you should know. I should have told you then, but I didn't want to come between you and your parents."

"My parents? What do they have to do with it? They never knew of our relationship." She raised a trembling hand to her forehead. *Or did they?*

"Actually, they did. I don't know how they found out. I'll probably never know. Your father tends to issue commands more than reveal his inner thoughts." A wry smile crossed his face, and he shook his head.

"That's true enough."

"That next day, after we were talking about colleges, your father summoned me to your house. He wanted me to come directly after school. Our meeting didn't last long. I guess it didn't need to, because I never got to say a word. He told me that I wasn't right for you and that I should stop spending time with you." He spread his hands wide. "What else was I to do, Hannah? I knew I wasn't good enough. He was only confirming the very reasons why we hadn't told anyone. My parents had died just a few years before, and my aunt and uncle were not exactly the same caliber as your family. I didn't have anything to offer you. No money. No status. No job prospects. I wasn't even sure how I was going to pay for college."

"Father told you to stay away from me?"

"Yes. But don't think ill of him. He wasn't harsh, just firm. And he was thinking of what he thought was best for you. A bad match can ruin lives."

"So you never talked to me again."

"I didn't know what else to do. I still saw you plenty. You just didn't see me."

Hannah's heart thudded against her chest, and she pressed her hands together. "I saw you at graduation, and you wouldn't look at me." She had blinked back tears for most of the ceremony, completely unable to enjoy the celebration of her huge accomplishment.

"Your father was at graduation, and I knew he'd have his eye on me. I didn't want to risk anything by even looking at you. I was a nobody from the wrong side of the tracks, as the saying goes. I didn't want to be on the outs with a wealthy and powerful man in the community."

"You could have found me, Derek. I didn't go far. You could have made it right." The rejection engulfed her, and she closed her eyes to stop the room from spinning around her.

"And what would have been the point? You would have had to choose between your family and me. I wasn't willing to put you in that position." He stood and went to get a bottle of water from the refrigerator.

If that was a signal that the conversation was over, she wasn't accepting it. She waited until he returned to his sofa and sipped his water. Then, she spoke in a hushed tone. "It's not societal position or amount of wealth that makes a man. It's who you are on the inside."

Quiet surrounded them as their tension-fraught discussion came to an abrupt halt. Hannah sighed. Maybe they could get some rest now before daylight appeared. Before another bad man with a gun shot at her.

But Derek sat forward, his elbows on his knees. "You do know how blessed you are to be adopted, right?"

"Blessed?"

"Definitely. I'm sure it's a shock, but based on what little you know about the circumstances of your birth, do you really think you would have been better off with your birth mother? On the run all the time?"

She hadn't thought of that. Would she even be alive right now? "Still, though, I've just barely found out I'm adopted and I'm on the run. Isn't there supposed to be a happy reunion with my birth parents? A discovery of how much we're alike and where I got the shape of my nose and why I'm so analytical? What about the part where they tell me they wish they could have kept me all along?"

"Where did you get all those ideas?" His chuckle was soft amid the background noises of the police station.

"I read. Sometimes it happens that way in novels." She paused, picking at a fingernail. "If my father is with the Mafia as you say, maybe he does wish he had kept me. I could have been a Mafia lackey. Or maybe still a lawyer. What Mafia family wouldn't want a good lawyer in the family?"

"Then even more reason to be glad your parents adopted you."

The man had a point. She pushed the blanket aside and sat up. Sleep wasn't going to come anytime soon.

When her birth mother had been forced to the decision that Hannah was safer with someone else, Father and Mother had stepped up and taken in a child they had never met. They didn't know her background, her medical history, her personality. But they took her home and loved her and protected her.

But turning Derek away? Telling him he wasn't right for her? Did Father really think that was in her best interests? And if Derek didn't think he was good enough, either, then why was he here? Why didn't he leave her in the lurch?

He was here because she was a job. An assignment. That was all. Once she was safe and the case closed, he would be gone.

Just like he had disappeared before.

And she would have a job for the summer and finish law school next year and become a do-gooder society spinster lawyer living with her mother and father.

She could live with that. Couldn't she?

Father. Her eyes went wide. She stared down at her wrist. "My watch." A gold image of the scales of justice sparkled against a black face.

"What about it?" Derek leaned forward to see it, fastening the cap back on his bottle of water.

She stretched out her arm to show him the watch. "Father sent me this today, remember? And the return address was a little odd because it just said *Dad,* and I don't call him *Dad.* But I was so eager for his approval that I didn't think anything more about it."

"You had it in your bag, and then, after you opened it, you've been wearing it ever since?"

Her palms slicked as she thought of the

possibility. Could it be a bug? The sender would have wanted her to accept the package without question, so he addressed it as if from her father, not knowing that she didn't call her father *Dad*. Hannah cut her eyes at him. "Yes."

"Let me have it. It might be a tracking device. How else would they have found you so quickly? How would they have found us at the library?"

She unfastened the band and handed the watch over, then followed him to the cabinets and watched him fumble through drawers until he found a plastic case with a set of small screwdrivers. Gently, he popped the back off of the watch. Inside, a tiny metal device lay nestled in the gears. Would it have eventually stopped the watch? It wouldn't have mattered, though. By that time, the thugs had probably planned to have eliminated her, which would conclude their need to track her.

Derek ran water in the kitchenette's sink as he pried the device out of the watch. He handed it back to her then dropped the tracker into the water. "If you still want the watch, it should be fine. Those guys ought not to be able to track you with that now." He paused, then turned to look at her. "But the device was still functional when we arrived here."

"So they probably know we're here?"

He simply nodded, his expression conveying all of the worst possibilities without a single word.

She inhaled deeply and took the watch, then sagged onto one of the sofas. Exhaling as she collapsed into the leather, she tucked the watch into her bag.

"I need to make a call." He made the call, and from hearing his end of the conversation, it seemed that he had called his supervisor. The conversation didn't last long after Derek mentioned destroying the tracking device. "Would the Mafia thugs come to a police station to find her? We're locked in and secure here."

After a moment of silence, Derek ended the call. He turned to her, an intensity burning in his dark eyes. "We need to go."

He didn't need to explain. She slipped on her shoes and grabbed her bag.

As Derek snagged a couple of water bottles from the refrigerator, the door to the break room opened. A uniformed officer came in. Derek glanced at him then returned his attention to Hannah, handing her the bottles to tuck into her bag.

Hannah clutched her bag and closed her eyes and tried her best to force her worries of the day out of her mind. Her favorite verse rang through her mind. *Do not worry about tomorrow, for tomorrow will worry about its own things. Sufficient for the day is its own trouble.*

Before she could repeat it a second time, the sound of feet scuffing on the floor broke into her reverie. A voice growled, "Let's go."

She popped her eyes open to find a gun pointed at her. She faltered back a step and watched as Derek, at the urging of the man in the officer's uniform, handed over his weapon. Her heart churned within her chest. They were supposed to be safe here. But this thug had somehow gotten his hands on an officer's uniform and security card and waltzed right into the station. Now, the man urged them toward the door.

Derek's lips were moving but no sound issued forth. Most likely, he was starting this next exploit with prayer, beseeching the Heavenly Father to protect and preserve them.

A moment later, they were outside and being ushered into the backseat of a two-door

Blazer, where another man already sat behind the wheel. The man who had taken Derek's SIG slammed the back of the seat into position and slid into the front passenger seat. As they pulled away from the station, the gray of early-morning light dispersed as the sun peeked over the horizon.

Hannah bit her lip. If only the office of the airport police wasn't at such a remote end of the terminal. If only it was later in the day, when more officers would be on duty. If only the thug hadn't been able to get his mitts on a uniform and security card somehow.

There was no point in wondering how it could have gone differently, or where she and Derek had gone wrong in their decision-making.

The entire ambush had lasted less than a minute, and they hadn't seen a single soul.

EIGHT

Hannah pushed hair off her forehead and wished she could flip the visor down to shield the morning sun. Instead, she shifted in her seat until the head of the guy in front of her blocked the glare.

The thug thumped the back of the seat. "Sit still." The menace in his voice sent shivers down her arms.

Derek maneuvered in his, holding the armrest as if he wanted to grab the nonexistent door handle for a quick escape. "Where we going, boys?" His tone held authority but without any threat.

The brute in the passenger seat turned to look at him. "Boys? You think we're pals now?" He cut his eyes toward Derek's weapon, which rested in the console between the two front seats, in front of the gearshift and out of Derek's reach. "If you had your SIG, you wouldn't be so friendly, would you?"

"It's just a simple question."

Hannah had to admit the thugs had planned it well. They'd swooped in during the quietest moment in the airport police station and taken them hostage. There was no way out now.

"If you must know, you're going to meet the girl's father. You've caused us so much trouble that he wants a few words before the end."

As the brute swiveled back to the front, Derek turned to stare at her, his eyebrows furrowed. He nodded toward the front, and the glare of the rising sun caught her eye again. Wherever they were headed, it was east.

Surely he was coming up with a plan to somehow get them out of the vehicle. Hannah's heart thumped against her rib cage, and she dabbed at the nervous perspiration that dotted her forehead. She forced herself to relax against the back of the seat. There was nothing she could do at this point in time, and there was no point in getting her blood pressure up.

She looked again at Derek, trying to judge his demeanor by his facial expression. Was he scared? Or was he plotting? But he only looked back at her with blankness, then he laid a warm but calloused hand over hers. She gripped his hand tightly, a desperate attempt to extract all the encouragement and support and strength conveyed in that simple touch.

A chuckle from the front rumbled through the vehicle. "Well, ain't that sweet?"

Hannah looked up to find a leering face peering at her from between the seats. She recoiled, drawing herself as far back as she could.

The thug in the passenger seat thumped the driver on the arm. "We got true love blossoming in the back." Sarcasm laced his words.

Derek blew out a harsh breath and stared out the window. Quiet engulfed them as the man in the passenger seat fell silent. As the vehicle changed lanes, she withdrew her hand. Derek didn't try to hold on to it.

Hannah swallowed over the lump that had formed in her throat at the coldness of her hands. At the prospect of never seeing Derek again. Before he'd reappeared and saved her life, she had put him out of her mind. But now that they were together again, albeit through necessary circumstances, she was forced to admit how much she had missed him. Could she still be in love with him after all these years?

She bit her lip to stop the tear that was beginning to form. She had her own plan. Her parents didn't exactly approve, and she could never buck them completely, never lose their good graces and their love. But she had to follow her heart into the law. And her pro bono law career would be about as much rebellion as any of them could tolerate. There would still be time in her schedule for garden parties and the country club. She couldn't bring Derek back into her life as well.

If they survived.

As they approached the other side of the city, still heading east, in the direction of Heartwood Hill, Hannah felt a nudge from Derek. She turned to see him staring at her with wide eyes and nodding his head toward the guys up front. She prayed that it was just as she had hoped, that he had a plan.

Keeping his hands low, he held them palms out, like a traffic cop signaling a driver to stop. Then, he motioned toward the door handle on the driver's side and then the passenger side and immediately moved both hands as if pushing forward.

Was he trying to communicate with her

without drawing the ire of their captors? Well, she would do her best to follow his lead when the time came. She nodded to him, but did she really understand it? They would only know in the moment of hopeful escape.

Their driver exited the interstate and turned south into Heartwood Hill. A couple of miles later, he drove through the small downtown and past the courthouse and turned into an abandoned parking lot between a set of two-story buildings.

"I know where we are," Hannah whispered to Derek. "And it's not good. Both of these buildings are empty now. One used to be a machine shop, and the other was a warehouse."

"That's right, missy." The driver spoke for the first time in the entire trip. "Time to get out."

As the two in the front reached for their door handles, Derek nodded forward and cut his eyes toward the guy in the passenger seat. Mimicking Derek's every move, Hannah quickly slid her hand inbetween the edge of the seat and the door. Her fingers found the lever that would release the back of the seat.

Suddenly, his plan took shape in her mind. As soon as the Blazer's door latch released, and just a split second after Derek grabbed for the lever, Hannah pulled the lever on her side and threw her entire body weight on the back of the front passenger seat. Next to her, Derek slammed against the back of the driver's seat. The seats simultaneously threw the men forward. Two separate thumping sounds heralded the thugs' heads hitting the windshield.

Grabbing another lever, Hannah and Derek slid the seats forward until their captors were pinned against the dashboard. Derek leaned into the middle of the front seats and grabbed his weapon from the console. At his head jerk toward the door, Hannah gave one final shove forward and crawled out of the backseat and onto the asphalt.

Derek ran around the back of the Blazer and grabbed her hand. Before he pulled her toward the corner of the building, she glanced back. A moan arose from the man in the passenger seat, but his eyes were closed.

"Come on," he urged her. "They're just dazed, so we better disappear. Could be more inside."

Hannah ran to keep up, not willing to let go of the firmness of his hand around hers. They dashed around the corner of the warehouse and down the block toward a main road. The clock tower of the courthouse rose above the trees another block over.

"There. I know security at the courthouse. It'll be safe." By the time they hit the sidewalk in front of the courthouse, they'd slowed to a walk.

Out of the corner of her eye, Hannah watched Derek stride beside the manicured bushes and pink flowers surrounding the building. It should have been exciting, having a handsome man walk with her and hold her hand. But this wasn't personal. As they approached the closest door and, hopefully, safety, at a brisk pace, he released her hand. He had thrown up a shield around himself, his expression blank and hardened, his arms taut, as he slipped back into his FBI special agent role. His demeanor looked casual, but Hannah knew he was wound up tight, ready to spring on anyone who appeared to be a threat.

Just inside the door, velvet ropes led them to a metal detector and two armed security officers. An X-ray security scanner for purses and briefcases and bags stood off to the side. She pulled her bag off her shoulder, but Derek swung out an arm to halt her.

With a grim look, he walked up to the

closest guard, his hand out. "Hey, Brandon. How're you doing?"

A look of surprise washed over the man's face and he eagerly shook Derek's hand. "Derek. It's been a long time. Heard you're FBI now."

Derek pulled out his badge, his SIG peeking out from under his shirt. "Yeah. I'm legit." He leaned in to Brandon and jerked his thumb in the direction from which they had come. "We had some trouble over at the old warehouse. Can you call for some uniforms to check it out? We're going to use the facilities and catch a breath."

"Sure." Brandon reached for a phone on a nearby stand. "You all right?"

Derek nodded. The guard waved them both through the metal detector, and Derek moved Hannah toward the staircase.

A wave of pride washed over her. Her high school sweetheart had matured into a strong, capable man who put others first. But as she glanced back at Brandon, her anxiety at their circumstances returned, and her stomach tied itself into a knot worthy of an experienced sailor.

If she could hold on to Derek's hand, she would be comforted. But she couldn't send the wrong signal, especially in front of people he knew and people she hoped to know someday soon. Instead, she just leaned close. "Do you think those guys after us would be able to get in here?"

He looked over at her, his mouth grim. "Doubtful. Brandon's a good officer. All of the security officers here are top-notch. I don't think even a Mafia heavy would be able to get a weapon inside."

"Really?"

"Yes. We ought to be relatively safe inside, but let's keep our eyes open. Just in case."

They approached the first turn of the wide marble staircase, and Hannah ran her hand over the smooth railing. On the second floor, she stepped into the restroom for a few minutes to splash water on her face and wash her hands.

As they ascended to the third floor of the courthouse, with just a few steps to go to a seating area where they could rest for a few moments, Derek nudged her. She followed his gaze only to be confronted by the malicious stare of a short, wiry man. The light in the hallway reflected off his balding head. He was not the man from the photo in the newspaper, but the way he glared at them made goose bumps crawl up Hannah's skin.

Derek slowed next to her, and she matched her pace to his. The man stepped slowly toward the stairs and moved in a menacing gait that made her pulse race. Hadn't Derek said they would be safe inside? If that guy was inside, who was waiting outside?

Her legs trembled as she stopped on the steps. Derek stared long and hard at the man, then turned, pulling her with him, and headed back down the way they had just come up. As they continued down, he picked up the pace, and she slid her hand along the railing to make sure she didn't trip and fall.

She risked a look behind. The wiry man hadn't turned the corner yet. If she kept her voice low, would Derek share his plan? "Where are we going?"

"Away from him."

The hallway on the second floor was empty, and Derek hurried her across to the opposite set of stairs. Perhaps they could get some help? Someone to stop him? But the courthouse seemed vacant. And what would they stop him for anyway? Glaring at someone was not a crime. As of yet, the wiry man had done nothing wrong.

"We'll get Brandon."

Yes, that was a good plan. More law enforcement.

But as they hit the first floor in a fast walk, another man approached them from the very door to which they were headed. He was a bulky, muscled man who wore a scowl as if it was his default setting.

She squeezed Derek's hand and her heart leaped into her throat. It suddenly didn't matter if Brandon was at his post or not.

"We're not going outside. Follow me and stay close. I think I remember something." Derek's voice was low, and he barely moved his lips.

With the burly man still halfway down the hallway, Derek drew her around a corner. Her shoes slid on the slick marble floor, and she grabbed at him with both hands to stay upright. A heavy, wooden, four-paneled door labeled Janitor stood to the left. Derek jerked the knob to yank it open. He pushed her inside and jumped in behind her.

He pulled the door closed quietly. Inky blackness enveloped them with only a sliver of light shining under the door. The acrid odor of cleaning chemicals assaulted her, and she leaned in to his cotton shirt to use it as a filter. She inhaled deeply of the fresh scent, of a clean breeze in the springtime.

Hannah rocked back on her heels. What was she doing getting so close to him? But then the nasty chemicals assailed her again, and she couldn't stop herself from leaning in to breathe in his scent again.

The sliver of light from under the door remained constant. Did that mean the man had not found them or even walked past the door? Derek pressed his ear to the door, and Hannah prayed his stillness meant that there was nothing to be heard. But a moment later, he pulled away.

"Here." He handed her his cell. "Flashlight."

She tapped the app, and the room glowed in the low light. He stepped toward a wall of wooden shelves laden with bottles of cleaners and disinfectants and paper towels. Moving items aside in a methodical fashion, he felt the wall behind, running his hands up and down the drywall. "Do you remember those rumors that circulated in high school?" His whisper echoed loudly in the small space.

"No. You mean about the courthouse?"

"Yeah, from our history teacher."

"I don't think I heard—"

"Shh." He held out a hand to cut her off, then pointed toward the bottom of the door.

Footsteps click-clacked slowly down the hallway. The echo rolled up and down the corridor and seemed to bang on the closet door.

The light that had crept in under the wooden door from the hallway was suddenly blacked out. Someone was out there, and it didn't appear to be the janitor.

Hannah froze. The flashlight still shone toward the shelves on the back wall. But it provided enough light to see that the doorknob began to turn.

He was here. At the door.

"Let's move it. Double time." Derek grabbed a rolling bucket and mop and pushed them toward Hannah. He felt steady and sure, and was thankful to be able to perform under pressure like this. Hannah received the mop bucket and gently placed them against the door. He nodded his agreement with the location and handed her a large, half-empty five-gallon bucket. Anything they could place against the door would not only impede the intruder's entry, even if just for a few moments, but also make a racket when he opened the door, drawing the attention of anyone nearby.

He continued to hand her large containers that had been sitting on the floor. As the space cleared, he ran his hands along the edges of the floor tiles. Surely there would be a finger-hold or a latch to grab on to, if the rumors were true.

If they weren't, then what? He didn't have the time to formulate a Plan B.

A poke in the shoulder made him spin around to see that the doorknob had stopped turning. Whoever was out there was ready to push in.

He reached for Hannah to pull her behind him. Her protection was the priority here, and he would go down to keep her safe if that was what was required of him.

Before he could grab her, though, she dodged toward a shelf of containers and unscrewed the lid of a large bottle. The stench of disinfectant filled the tiny area. The door opened, and Hannah tossed the nasty chemical concoction in the face of the man in the doorway.

It was the bulky man from around the corner, and Hannah had judged his height perfectly. The liquid hit his eyes, and he stumbled backward. His arms flailed toward his face as if to scrub away the burn. Derek heard a low moan under the splash of the chemicals.

He yanked the door shut again. They couldn't leave the courthouse now, but they needed to get out. There was too much chance that the wiry man had exited the building to wait for them, perhaps with the other Mafia thugs if they had avoided capture. And if they were outside, they most likely had weapons.

Dropping to his knees on the floor, Derek shoved aside the remaining bottles on the bottom shelf and pulled away the boards that had been nailed up in a flimsy manner to make shelves for the storage closet. His fingers quickly found a hold on the wall itself, and he pulled away a piece of cheap paneling to reveal a trapdoor about three feet high and two feet wide.

"Eureka!" As much as he wanted to shout in jubilation, he forced himself to keep his voice to an excited whisper.

Hannah peeked around him, her hair brushing against his face and the scent of her shampoo tickling his nose. "We're free!" She leaned toward him and landed a kiss on his cheek.

His heart in overdrive, he leaned back on his heels. "Not yet, but we're closer than we were."

The tunnel inside looked like the movie images of a mine shaft, with packed dirt walls and support beams adding strength to the ceiling. It sloped down steeply, and if the rumors were correct, it angled under the street and reopened…somewhere. Whoever had dug it obviously hadn't spent a lot of time, effort or money on it. It was purely functional, but he was good with that, considering the circumstances.

Before they could make their escape though, he ought to throw those thugs off their trail. The noise outside the door had subsided—the guy with the chemicals in his face was probably fleeing to the washroom to find relief in clean, clear water. Derek opened the door slowly to find the hallway empty. He grabbed the mop and a couple of the large bottles and, as quietly as possible, arranged them on the floor in the hallway to make it look as if they had taken off from the closet in haste.

Leaving the door ajar, he turned back into the closet and urged Hannah into the tunnel. "Ladies first."

"I know this creepy tunnel that's probably full of spiders is better than facing that guy out there, but you'll be right behind me. Right?" Her voice wobbled in the quiet of the closet.

"Definitely."

She crawled in and descended a rough set of stairs until she could stand upright, then turned and waited for him, shining the cell-phone flashlight toward the ground in his direction.

Derek backed into the tunnel. Reaching through the door, he hoisted the shelves onto the brackets and pulled what supplies were within his grasp back into place on the shelves. The closet still had bottles and brooms out of place and all over the floor, but perhaps whoever found it would think those things had been scattered in their haste to get out.

The last thing was to replace the paneling that created the wall and close the trapdoor. He backed down the stairs since he was too big to turn around in the narrow passageway. At the bottom, he inched around and finally stood upright. He put a finger to his lips to indicate that she should keep quiet and shuffled past her to take the lead through the tunnel.

Several yards in, Hannah put a hand on

his shoulder blade. He stopped and turned to hold up a hand, listening for any indication of being followed. Only complete and chilling silence filled the space around them. He nodded to her that it was okay to talk. Perhaps a little conversation would de-creepify the tunnel a bit.

"How did you know about this tunnel?"

"I took a chance that the rumors were true. Good thing they were, huh?"

"I never heard any rumors about a secret underground tunnel." She edged forward, glancing around at the walls and ceiling, clearly uncertain as to the safety of their location.

"We had different history teachers. This courthouse dates back over one hundred and fifty years, clear back to the Civil War. Mr. Goode loved to talk about a supposed tunnel that was used to hide and transport passengers on the Underground Railroad. One end was at the courthouse, but no one knew where the other end came out." He placed a hand on her upper back to push her along gently. "The thought was that a couple of the men who worked on the construction of the building in the 1850s were involved with the Railroad, so they dug the tunnel to help runaway slaves avoid recapture."

"That's pretty cool, then, that this tunnel is here for such noble purposes."

"Well, there was also a rumor that a judge in the 1970s used it to hide his criminal activities. I never heard exactly what."

"Oh."

"But we've redeemed it. We're using it again for running away from the bad guys."

She glanced back and he forced a smile for her. But a muscle twitched in his temple that he prayed she couldn't see in the semi-darkness. They seemed safe now, and he was grateful the rumors had proven accurate. But he had told the truth, that no one seemed to know where the tunnel ended. What if it had been sealed up years ago and they had to go back the way they came? He had been plotting off the top of his head back in the closet. He had no Plan B. This wasn't Hogan's Alley back in Quantico, the mock town the academy used for training, and these thugs weren't actors hired for a training exercise. This was real life. These were real criminals. He better keep his head in the game.

He scrubbed his hand over his stubbled chin, then reached for the cell flashlight from

Hannah and stepped around her to take the lead. A wave of relief washed over her face as she stepped behind him.

"This tunnel can't go too far, probably just across the street."

They approached a curve, and as Derek rounded the bend, a cobweb engulfed him and wrapped itself around him. It stuck to his arms and neck, and he clawed at it to free himself from the clingy, sticky tendrils. He grimaced, glad he wasn't facing Hannah. As slithery as it felt against his skin, better him than her.

After a long straightaway and dodging a few more cobwebs, the light shone on what seemed to be the end of the tunnel. A wall of rough-hewn boards rose up in front of them. Derek handed the light back to Hannah, dug his fingers in around the end of one at shoulder height and pulled. It wiggled, and with a little more effort, came loose, bringing clods of dirt down with it.

A brick wall stood behind it.

Sniffling sounded behind him, the light wobbling on the bricks. He turned to find Hannah's shoulders shaking as she struggled to hold back tears. "What are we going to do?" Her voice was hoarse with emotion.

As much as he wanted to gather her in his

embrace, stroke her hair and comfort her, that wouldn't get them out of the tunnel. "We keep going." He put a hand on her shoulder and squeezed gently, whispering a prayer for a good outcome.

There had to be a way through that brick wall. He turned back and grabbed another board. It came loose and revealed more brick, but this time he spied what looked like a handhold in between bricks. He pulled again, and with another board loose, another handhold was exposed.

"I think I see something. Shine the light over here." He gestured toward the top handhold. The light followed his hand, and he leaned in for a closer look, his heart pounding loudly in the quiet of the tunnel. "See? If I can get enough fingers in here—" he fit his fingers into the open space "—and then pull, I think it might come loose." He carefully yanked on a piece of brick.

He didn't want everything to come loose at once since he didn't know what was behind the brick. But with a gentle pull, not one brick but a sheet of brick inched out of the space.

Behind him, Hannah sighed. "This is good, right?"

He pulled again, and a large section eased

out into his hand, revealing a dark, empty space behind it. "Almost anything would be better than the tunnel." He reached for the light. "Let's find out."

The light swept through the hole. They had come to what looked to be a cellar, with brick walls and metal shelving units filled with boxes and supplies. "I think this will work, but the opening isn't big enough to fit through yet."

He passed the light back to Hannah and pulled on another section of brick. This one was stuck in more tightly, and he strained to yank it free. But a moment later, it came loose, and he fell back against the dirt wall of the tunnel. He stood and brushed himself off, then, moving aside a rolling shelving unit, he clambered through the hole and into the cellar. Turning back for Hannah, he took the cell from her and grasped her arm to steady her as she crawled through.

A flip of the light switch revealed a storage room filled with restaurant supplies like boxes of foam cups, to-go boxes and packages of paper napkins. Wooden stairs led the way up. Hannah inhaled deeply, and Derek followed. The earthy scent of the tunnel had been replaced by the stale, musty odor of cardboard and brick. But over that, there was another, more pleasing aroma.

A smile quickly arched across Hannah's face. "Do you smell that? Coffee."

He did smell it. The scent of brewing beans quickly overcame the other aromas. It was the scent of safety and tranquility. "I think I know where we are. We've crossed Main Street, and we're in the cellar of that coffee shop and restaurant that's on the square on the other side of the street from the courthouse."

"The Green Bean."

"That's the place." He inhaled deeply one more time, savoring the aroma and willing his pulse back to a normal rate. "Unfortunately, I think we better keep going. I don't think those guys found the tunnel. They would have caught up with us by now. But we can't stand still. Plus, the proprietor of The Green Bean probably wouldn't be happy to find two strangers hiding out in his storage room."

"Let's get this put back, then." Apparently invigorated by freedom and the hope of coffee, Hannah tried to lift a section of the brick to replace the wall.

"I'll get it." He fit the brick sections back into place and rolled the shelving unit to its original location, hiding the holds in the brick.

"It looks good. I don't think anyone will ever notice." Hannah straightened and brushed her hands off. "So now what? Can we get a coffee? And I think I smell pastries, too. We never had breakfast."

"Coffee and a danish sound terrific." Derek slapped his hands against his khakis, brushing the dirt and brick dust from his hands and his clothes. He could really use a shower about now, too, but there simply wasn't time. Hannah was safe, yes, but those thugs were still somewhere around the square, most likely looking for them. They couldn't live like moles, hiding underground. They needed to rise to the surface, but only with extreme caution.

He stepped closer to pick up a package of napkins that had fallen on the floor. When he rose from replacing them on the shelf, he was inches from her. A smudge of dust from the tunnel clung to her cheek, and he brushed it away with his thumb. Before he could stop himself, he slid his other arm around her waist and pulled her close.

Maybe it was the danger they had just come through, or maybe it was the probability of danger when they rose to street level. Maybe it was the hope for a future together that was working its way into his heart. But he needed to hold her close, to inhale her scent, to reassure himself that she was warm and real and right here with him. The memory of her had not left him for the past ten years. Now she was here, and he was here, and there might not come a moment like this again.

As much as he didn't want to admit it, he was falling in love with her all over again.

She gasped at his arm around her, her lips parting slightly in surprise. But she didn't pull away. "Shouldn't we go?" she whispered.

"In a minute. We're safe for now." He leaned in closer, his breath mingling with hers, ready to claim another kiss. It had been nearly ten years since the last one, the only kiss they had ever shared. A small part of his brain hammered at him to leave her alone, to leave that kiss in the past, where it belonged. As he hovered over her parted lips, he silenced his thoughts, lowering his head toward hers.

"Whoa, what's going on here?" A loud voice startled him, and Hannah jumped back, out of his arms.

A kid who couldn't have been more than sixteen years old stood at the bottom of the stairs. Thick blond hair fell over his eyes, and he wore a black apron tied over his beige cargo pants and black polo. *The Green Bean* was embroidered at the top of the apron.

Derek stepped back and cleared his throat, straightening his shoulders and rising up to his full height, which was a few inches more than the teenager.

The teenager cowered slightly, but not enough to please Derek. "How'd you get in here? You're not supposed to be here."

"Relax, Sparky. I'll let you in on a little secret." He whisked out his badge and flipped open the cover with a flourish.

Sparky stepped back, his eyes racing to the weapon in the shoulder holster that was revealed when Derek reached for his credentials. "Whoa. FBI?" He let his gaze roam over Derek, then he glanced down at his own scrawny biceps. In a moment of silence, he stepped back toward the stairs. "Wa-want a coffee?"

Derek suppressed a grin. He held out his hand to Hannah, ushering her toward the stairs, and they followed the kid up and into a back hallway. A quick glance out the nearest window revealed only a Dumpster and a back parking lot with a single compact car in it.

Sparky led them into the restaurant and sat

them at a table near the back, half behind a ficus tree. "This okay?"

"Fine. Thanks." He held out the chair that sat the farthest behind the tree for Hannah, then surveyed the dining area and the picture window that looked out on the town square. A dozen or more patrons dressed in professional garb sipped beverages and nibbled sandwiches, and only one had even noticed when they had appeared from the back, just glancing at them from half-lidded eyes. Another employee stood behind the counter, filling a display case with cookies.

The teenager returned a moment later, two coffees in hand, a design decorating the top of each beverage. He left them on the table, a nervous glance shot at Derek and a hint of a smile aimed at Hannah.

Derek scooted his chair a tad to the left to get a better view of the courthouse and the street between them. If he could get visual contact with the Mafia heavies, he would feel much better about their safety.

Hannah sipped her coffee, the motion drawing his attention away from his surveillance. "Shouldn't we hide?"

He forced his attention back to the street. *Focus, man.* "We are hiding. In plain sight.

We're just sitting here having a coffee, being normal. Who's going to notice us? But maybe we should pull out our phones to look more like everyone else." He shot a smile at her, willing her to relax. He was tense enough for the both of them. "From this spot, we'll see them first anyway."

Sparky returned and placed a plain chocolate-chip cookie in front of Derek, but he turned to Hannah and handed her one in the shape of a heart with a dollop of pink icing. His face was the same color as the icing, and he stuttered out, "Would you like a c-c-cookie?"

Hannah flashed a dazzling smile at him, and Derek's own heart flip-flopped. Sparky's color deepened, and he turned right into the branches of the ficus. He pushed it aside and disappeared again. Derek hid his smile at the boy's awkwardness around a beautiful woman, but he couldn't blame him. Hannah had made him splutter plenty when he was a teenager. She still would if he didn't force himself to stay focused on the task at hand.

A man holding a hand to his face walked by the window of the coffee shop. Derek jerked back, farther behind the tree. It was the bulky man who had cornered them in the closet. His eyes were probably still stinging from the chemicals Hannah had thrown at him. At the sound of a shout, he turned, and the scrawny man ran up to him. Neither of them looked like the man in the newspaper who was, most likely, Hannah's birth father.

Derek nudged Hannah and nodded toward the window. She followed his gaze and visibly started when she saw their attackers. To her credit, she didn't make a noise or get up to run, so as not to draw attention to them.

Should he take a photo? It seemed a big risk that might expose them. Before he could decide and retrieve his phone, the two continued on together outside Derek's view.

At least he'd had a good, long look, and Hannah probably had a mental image as well.

The question that plagued him was where was Hannah's birth father? Wouldn't he be close by, giving the orders? Supposedly, their abductors had been taking them to him, but he had yet to be seen or identified.

"So what happens next?" Hannah had sunk back into her chair, the cookie and coffee abandoned on the table.

"We continue to lie low." He sipped his coffee to show her all was well. "Let the other agents do their jobs. If the local police have caught those guys that took us from the airport, that would help. But the one time we had them, as they exited the parking garage at the library, they escaped."

"We can't just let them go. They're guilty," she said as she picked up her cup.

"As much as I admire your zest for justice, Hannah, there's nothing I can do at this moment in time." But a glance at the front of the restaurant froze the blood in his veins.

The two thugs were back, and they were looking in the café window.

NINE

"They're back."

Hannah froze with her coffee cup in midair as Derek's throaty whisper reached her ears. Without moving her head, she lifted her eyes to see the two men framed in the window.

"Just sit still."

She didn't need Derek's instruction to know not to move. The men weren't exactly tyrannosauruses who saw only things that moved. Staying still wouldn't make them invisible. Yet, any movement on their part could draw attention to them.

The thugs turned to stand with their backs to the window, probably staring at the courthouse across the street. One was on the phone, perhaps getting orders from Hannah's birth father. What would she give to be able to listen in on that sinister conversation?

Derek moved slowly to pull out his phone,

and then pretended to scroll, all while furtively watching the men. Hannah copied him, watching them from under her eyelashes as best she could from her position behind the ficus tree. The thug on the phone apparently ended the call because he put the phone in his pocket. Then, the two turned in a circle, surveying the area around them. But as they glanced in the café window, they continued turning.

Hannah wanted to sag in relief at not being noticed, but fear had sunk its claws into her spine, and she found she couldn't relax. "What about going back through the tunnel?" There was no way the guys outside could hear her on the inside amid the hubbub of the lunch crowd, but she couldn't force her voice above a whisper.

"No. I don't think that's going to be necessary. Anyway, can you imagine the ruckus we could cause if we suddenly popped out of the janitor's closet?" He tossed a smile in her direction, and it had the intended effect. She sat back in her chair and sipped her lukewarm coffee.

"How do we get out of here, then? And when we do get out of this coffee shop and away from the courthouse, then where do we go?" It was beginning to seem an impossible situation, and it hadn't even been twenty-four hours. Would she *ever* be safe again?

Derek sipped his coffee. Was he trying to buy some time? Hannah was beginning to wonder if he knew what he was doing. Yes, she trusted him, but trust didn't always come doubt-free.

The large group of office employees who had filled the tables toward the front began to stand, one by one, and move toward the register to pay their individual bills. Hannah nodded toward the crowd. "What now? They were shielding us from street view, and now everyone is leaving."

A smile ignited Derek's face, and his dimples deepened, as his face lit with an idea. "They can still shield us. Get your last sip, and grab your bag." He caught Sparky's eye and signaled him over to the table. "What do we owe you?"

The teen glanced at Hannah, his cheeks pinking. "Nothing, sir. I got this."

Derek stood and clapped him on the shoulder. "We appreciate it." He retrieved his wallet and handed the boy a card. "If you ever have interest in the FBI, shoot me an email."

A huge grin spread across his face. "Thank you, sir."

Hannah lifted her bag across her shoulder and fell in behind Derek's long strides toward the crowd that was now filing out the door.

Derek took the door handle from another woman and gestured Hannah through. "I'll be right behind you."

She nodded and stepped through, mixing into the crowd. Out on the sidewalk, she glanced back. Derek had let another couple of women through the door, then fell in beside the two men at the rear of the crowd.

A woman who looked about Hannah's age walked next to her, wearing a smart black A-line skirt with a pink blouse and a coordinating scarf. Maybe if she started a conversation, she would look more like she belonged. The men were looking for a single woman, perhaps with a single man. They might not even glance at a crowd of professionally dressed people.

She summoned her courage and offered a compliment, the best way to start a conversation with someone she didn't know. "I love your scarf."

The woman turned to her, her eyebrows scrunched in confusion. A moment of silence passed between them, and Hannah began to wonder if this plan of Derek's would work.

But then the woman spoke. "Thank you."

Hannah found herself scrambling for what to say next. Her new companion paused, taking a long look at Hannah. "I got it at that consignment shop in town."

Whew. They could talk about shopping. "That one on Maple Avenue?"

The woman nodded, her eyebrows not relaxing.

"I haven't been in there. Do they have a good selection?" Hannah kept her face toward her companion, but she wondered if she should look around for Derek or the bad guys.

"I think so."

They stopped at the light, waiting for the Walk signal. The crowd bunched around them, and Hannah, looking at the ground, spied Derek's shoes a couple of people over. She breathed deeply. Perhaps fresh air would help her think clearly. "What are their Saturday hours? I'm so busy during the week that I don't have time to shop until the weekend."

"I know what you mean. Making those ends meet." Her companion's facial features relaxed, as the woman apparently accepted this stranger who was making conversation. "They're open all day on Saturday. You should be able to find a time to drop in."

The light changed, and the crowd moved on, Hannah keeping pace. They crossed the street and walked past the courthouse, toward a two-story office building on the opposite street.

As they stepped onto the sidewalk, now half a block from the Callahans' office building, Derek appeared close by, but not right next to her. He nodded at her, then toward the Callahans' office. She said goodbye to her companion.

The woman waved. "Nice talking to you."

"Likewise." Her stomach lurched as she stepped away, alone for the first time since leaving the coffee shop. Derek was following, perhaps a couple of yards behind. But she still dared to look around, hoping her expression was casual enough to convince any observer that she was simply admiring the flowers. A man in a suit was just coming out of the courthouse, but he didn't seem menacing and didn't look at her at all.

A few minutes later, she pulled open the door to the office building and stepped into its marbled coolness. She quickly moved to the side, away from the glass doors and the street view. Derek followed right behind, pushing the door closed behind him and moving to her side.

"You all right?"

She nodded, swallowing past the dryness in her throat.

"I don't see any evidence of it, but it is possible they're monitoring the Callahans' offices. I don't want to stay long." Derek stared again out the front door, then cupped her elbow and steered her toward the elevators. "We'll just keep thinking. And praying."

In the third-floor office suite, Mallory Callahan registered surprise to see Hannah again. "You're back sooner than I expected. Everything's all right, then?"

Hannah turned to Derek for some help with an explanation, but he was silent. When she didn't answer, Mallory gestured to a client chair. "Everything is not all right?"

Hannah sank into the chair. Derek followed to the other chair. She squeezed her eyes shut, but a renegade tear escaped and betrayed her difficulty. "No. It's not all right. There's been nothing but trouble since I left here yesterday."

Mallory's eyebrows shot up. "What's happened? Are you safe now?"

"We obviously made it here all right, from The Green Bean, so I think we're safe." Derek reached over to take her hand.

Despite the flicker of question in Mallory's eyes at his gesture, Hannah didn't push him away. She was too desperate for something solid to hold on to. "It's a long, complicated story, but basically we've been on the run since we left here yesterday." Hannah filled her boss in on what had transpired as Derek added details to the narrative.

As they concluded the tale, she brushed a stray hair off her forehead then laid her hand in her lap, an effort to look professional. Was it really just a few weeks ago that she started her summer position here? Yet today, here she was, on the run and feeling disheveled without even a change of clothes. She would never take for granted her shower or her closet again.

Mallory sat forward, leaning her forearms on the desk, a knowing look in her eyes as she made eye contact with Hannah. "Good thing you have a dashing and gallant protector."

Derek withdrew his hand from hers, the disappearance of the warmth and firmness leaving her cold and empty. But the heat of a blush crept up her neck and into her cheeks.

Her face was probably flaming red. "Yes" was all she could choke out.

"Lots of people interested in contact with their birth parents start with the online registry. However, if your parents haven't registered, and it seems from the circumstances that they would not have, then that won't help you. It's not an overnight process anyway, so at this point in time, you probably just need to sit tight and stay safe."

"Father said that there was some sort of danger surrounding my adoption, but he wasn't sure what. Now, I'm getting worried about my birth mother. Since this all seems to be connected, what kind of trouble might she be in right now?"

Derek leaned forward. "Obviously, we don't know her. But considering the circumstances of her choices in giving you up for adoption, she's probably pretty tough and able to handle herself. And we have agents searching for her, to protect her as well."

Mallory nodded in agreement. "I'd say that's a fair assessment. Now what about you? How are you taking the new knowledge of being adopted? I know a good counselor if you want a referral. That's a big chunk of news to digest." Her face softened with an empathetic smile.

"My parents didn't want to admit it at first. Even though I understand that they were trying to keep me safe, it hurt to know that they had kept a secret from me for so long." She released a long, quavering breath, fighting back tears. "And then they talked on and on about the social circles they live and work in. I don't see how that matters. I'm their daughter. Aren't I more important than a business colleague or a friend at the country club?"

"My parents divorced when my sister and I were in high school, and it felt like my father didn't love me anymore. But eventually, I saw that that wasn't true. We don't always understand the things that happen in our lives, Hannah, but we need to keep trusting God and stay focused on His will for us, not turning to the left or to the right."

"That's exactly right." Derek's soft voice wrapped around her.

"What about looking at it from their perspective? You know the society they live in better than I do. Are the people really that way?"

Hannah turned that question around in her mind, letting events and people from her childhood and high school years float through her mind's eye. "I've seen some heinous behavior in that circle. A young man I went to preparatory school with met and married a girl from the local high school. She was sweet and smart and friendly, but she wasn't from one of *our* families. The boy was told that in no uncertain terms his parents disapproved of her. He married her anyway, and although his parents haven't broken with him completely, they are cold and distant and he's shunned from family activities and communication." Her parents would never treat her like that. Hannah was sure of that. But to see them treated in that manner from their so-called friends? She wouldn't be able to do anything that might cause that to happen to them.

"So they really were protecting you," Mallory said.

A hush fell over the office.

"They love you. Profoundly."

Hannah's heart swelled with affection for the people she called Mother and Father. "Yes. I think they do."

Derek inhaled deeply, a renewed vigor to keep Hannah safe coursing through his veins. Despite the difficulties he had had with her father, Hannah's relationship with her parents was worth fighting for. He wouldn't be able to face himself in the mirror if something happened and her parents had to suffer the loss of a child. He let out the breath. Who was he kidding? He couldn't bear to lose Hannah, either.

"I know I said we were safe, but we ought not stay in one place too long right now."

Hannah turned to him, her pretty brown eyes wide with worry. "All right. Where to?"

"I want to talk to Reid for a moment. Consult with another law enforcement officer."

He stood, and Hannah followed. They said goodbye to Mallory, then headed down the hallway to Reid's office.

"What about tracking through your phones?" Reid's first question was one Derek had already thought of.

"No. I've checked, and there's nothing that I can see. I did find one in a watch that Hannah received through the mail. The package said it was from *Dad*, but she calls her dad *Father*. Hannah was rather surprised, but I found the device and destroyed it last night. I think we're clean now."

"Best be on the lookout then. They won't give up. There are probably a couple of thugs with eyes on this place right now, waiting for you two to emerge."

His heart sunk to his stomach. He'd been thinking that exact thing, and it was not reassuring to hear Reid confirm it.

"What about a vehicle?"

"We don't have one now. I was going to rent something at the airport, but obviously that didn't pan out."

Reid held out his hand, palm open and up. "You'll take mine. I'm parked around front, but I'll go get it. I don't look anything like you, and they aren't searching for a single male. I'll drive it around back."

"I can't take your car."

"You can, and you will. It's the least I can do. Besides, that Cherokee can handle a little action. She still has plenty of maneuvers left in her, but I'll pray it doesn't come to that."

"Thanks."

As Reid took off through the office's back door, Hannah dug into her bag to extract a tissue. Exhaustion etched all over her pretty face, she moved to the window and stared down at the parking lot. "So, we're going back on the road?"

"Soon. Right now, I think you need to move away from the window. Just to be safe."

He held her upper arm and gently steered her to an interior wall of the office.

But when he had positioned her away from sight, he didn't—couldn't—let go. They had peace and quiet, if only for a moment. Grasping her other arm, he turned her toward him, and she collapsed against him. He encircled her in his embrace, stroking her hair and praying that it would ease away her exhaustion and frustration and fear.

With his parents deceased and his aunt and uncle uninterested, it had been years since Derek had felt the warmth and comfort of physical touch. It was a balm to his soul. How he had missed that human connection, and now he was here, again, with Hannah.

She lifted her head, a question in her eyes. But before she could speak, Derek touched his lips to hers, a gentle inquiry that zinged to his toes. He pulled away while he still had the self-control, overwhelmed by her beauty and the effort it took to catch his breath. She gazed up at him, apparently not appalled at his liberties, but not seeking another kiss, either.

"Do you think there's any—?" He cut himself off. He wanted to ask if she thought there was any chance for a future together, if her father would be more accepting of him now, if she could ever care for him again. But what would be the point? Just to hear again that it couldn't work?

Hannah swayed away, a pink tinge to her cheeks. "Any what?"

Derek cleared his throat. "Any chance for rain?" He peered out the window. "No, I think we'll be fine." He took a large step away and steered her toward the door while filling his lungs with oxygen that he prayed would clear his mind.

Hannah hitched her purse on her shoulder. "Time to go?"

"Reid is probably here with his vehicle." He wasn't sure where he would drive, but he'd figure it out on the way.

They grabbed the elevator and stepped inside. Derek pushed the button for the first floor, more than a little frustrated with himself. Would he ever have the courage to broach the topic of renewing their relationship? He shifted his weight from one leg to the other, but nothing eased his discomfort.

A ding signaled their arrival at the first floor. As the doors opened, Derek looked out, both ways, then stepped out with Hannah following close behind. The lobby was clear, and he turned right toward the parking lot, where Reid would pull up his Cherokee.

"Derek!"

He spun to see the burly man from the courthouse with his meaty paws on Hannah. The man clamped his hand over her mouth and dragged her around the corner from the elevator.

Adrenaline spiked through Derek, his skin tingling with the rush to high alert as he drew his SIG and followed Hannah. As he turned the corner, a service door out to the side of the building rose up before him. He opened the door slowly, but before he could open it enough to see what was on the other side, a crack sounded. Pain ripped through his arm as well as his heart. What would they do to her? He released the door and grabbed the site of the wound, blood sticking against his fingers. A glance at the wound revealed that the bullet had only grazed him, and he returned his focus to finding Hannah. He had to save her, even if it was the last thing he did.

He cracked the door again, keeping himself shielded behind it. When no other shots were fired, he opened it farther. The thugs were forcing Hannah into a large SUV in an alley behind the office building. His gut clenched at the thought of those heavies with their hands on her. She caught sight of him as they were pushing her head into the vehicle. A loud gasp tore through the air, her eyes locked on his bloody wound.

The wiry man turned back and aimed his weapon at Derek. But someone called to him from inside the SUV, and he jumped in, slamming the door. As the vehicle moved away, Derek stepped out to the alley, desperate to see which direction they headed. His breath puffed in short spurts as panic threatened to overtake him.

A moment later, Reid tore around the corner in his Cherokee. He squealed to a stop and stepped out. "I heard the shot and figured they were at the other door out of the building." His gaze swept up and down the alley. "Where's Hannah?"

Derek raced around to the driver's side. "They have her. I need to go." He slipped into the seat, gripping the wheel and throwing the vehicle into Drive. A second rush of adrenaline pulsed through his arteries, and he pushed the Cherokee out to the main road, turning in the same direction they had taken Hannah.

TEN

Hannah couldn't tell if the man driving was eager to finish off whatever they were going to do to her, or if he was just a maniacal driver, but the shops and galleries and restaurants along County Line Road sped past at a rate that made her eyes jiggle. The bright afternoon sun was another irritant, but when she turned her face to the interior of the vehicle, she was assaulted with the view of the guys who had kidnapped her and her stomach churned as if she might be sick. As they left the business district and headed out into the countryside, clouds began to gather to the west. A storm was brewing, and rain would begin soon.

Dread paralyzed her, but she managed to squeak out a request to crack the window to let in fresh air. The driver grunted and lowered her window a half inch. The sounds of late spring in Indiana filtered in, the soothing music of tree frogs and mother birds chirping as they gathered for their young. Tiny sprouts of corn had pushed up and unfurled new leaves, and the earthy smell of warm soil sifted in from freshly plowed and planted fields.

Indiana had been her home for as long as she could remember, but had it always been her home state? She didn't even know where her life had started, but perhaps she would find out soon. The two men in the vehicle were the men they had seen in the courthouse, and they had remained silent. No answers would be forthcoming from them, either. As much as she cared about her own safety, she had seen blood on Derek's sleeve. He had been shot, but she had no idea how bad it was. Could it have been fatal? Would she ever see him again? Ever get the chance to tell him that she loved him? A tear slipped down her cheek, and she swiped it away with the back of her hand. She had fallen for him all over again, and now any hope for a relationship had been dashed almost before it had even begun.

She needed to stay strong for Derek. To survive this and to make all his efforts worthwhile. She turned to the man next to her in the backseat. "How much longer until we're there?"

He remained silent without even a glance in her direction.

"Where are we going?" The breeze from the window blew hair in her face, and she pulled back some strands to tuck behind her ear.

Still no answer.

"Am I going to meet my birth father?"

That question elicited a sneer from her seat companion, but he returned his attention to the front without an answer.

Her window powered up, and she glanced at the driver to see his finger on the controls. There went her fresh air.

About forty-five minutes outside of Indianapolis, the driver turned off the highway, and the sign for Crooked Branch Park rose tall. As they passed through the unmanned gate and into the heavily wooded park, a shiver crept up Hannah's spine. She licked her dry lips and bowed her head to utter a silent prayer for protection and safety. Derek had been well-armed and knew how to use his weapons. But he wasn't here. And if he was ever outgunned, what would all of that training and experience matter anyway?

If only she had some training. A weapon, at least. But she'd always been too busy with her studies to bother with it. Well, weapon or not, she had the best protection a woman could have—the protection of God Almighty.

Would she meet her birth father at the end of this road? Did it matter anymore? She already knew who she was, what she was doing and why. Her faith in God had led her to those discoveries, no matter what her past had been. The news that she was adopted had been a shock, but if she had known all about her adoption and birth family growing up, would she not be in law school, on a course to a life of charitable giving, unmarried and alone? No, she had to admit, if only to herself. Law school was God's will for her. Knowledge of her birth parents would not have changed that.

She clenched her hands together. She would rely on God the Father like she never had before. He was the One who knew what was best, all the time.

The SUV turned a couple of times before the road led them to a deserted picnic pavilion with several trailheads. The driver pulled into a parking spot next to another large SUV. Hannah scanned the woods around them, but didn't see any sign of help. Would this be her last breath?

She grabbed her bag as the thug in the backseat pulled her out his door, his fingers pressing into her bicep.

The driver led them to trail five, a narrow, grassy path. They were forced to walk single file with Hannah in the middle. She stared at the back of the head in front of her with an occasional glance around. But memorizing her surroundings was useless. What she wouldn't give to be following behind the man with the broad shoulders, quick reflexes and FBI training. But he was compromised, no one else knew where she was and her grave was probably just a few yards down the path. Large boulders sat on either side of the trail, and the shadowed sun was blotted out by thick overhead foliage. Happy little buttercups bloomed by the trail, a stark contrast to the somber moment that was surely coming.

The packed-dirt path deep in the woods led around one of the largest boulders Hannah had ever seen and then widened into a clearing. She stumbled over a root sticking out of the ground and, unable to regain her balance, she fell into the clearing.

The burly thug yanked her to her feet.

A woman who was an older version of the photo in the newspaper stepped from behind a boulder. A stricken expression on the woman's lined face tore at Hannah, and she longed to rush forward to hug the woman who must be her birth mother.

A thick hand on her shoulder held her in her spot as a man stepped from behind the woman. Black hair with a salting of gray fell over his forehead, and he stared at Hannah with small black eyes. He held a gun pointed at the woman.

"Susan?" Hannah whispered.

Her birth mother nodded, a lone tear trickling down her drawn face. Hannah touched a hand to her own face and found that it was damp.

"See? I knew we would all be reunited someday. One happy family." A sinister smile snaked across the man's face, twisting his expression. "Come give your dear old dad a kiss."

So this was it. The reunion no one had dreamed of. Her birth mother staring at her, a mixture of what seemed like grief and love in her eyes. And her birth father held a gun to the poor woman.

He signaled to the thug near Hannah to join him on the other side of the small clearing, and she was left standing alone, facing the barrel of the weapon her own birth father pointed at her.

She caught a motion in the woods out of the corner of her eye. It must have drawn her birth father's attention as well, as he moved to the side of the clearing. "Come out, hero boy," he called into the woods.

Derek stepped out from behind a boulder, his hands empty. His bloody shirt stuck to him, but he held his wounded arm steady, and Hannah prayed that that meant he was not seriously injured. Keeping his focus trained on the men with guns, Derek joined Hannah and grasped her hand. Comfort and encouragement shot up Hannah's arm and straight to her heart.

"So, here we all are. Our happy family, plus now the boyfriend." A jeer marked the man's face. "You apparently found the tracking device in the watch I sent you. And then you gave my guys the slip at the courthouse. What else could I do but invite you here? I wanted to meet my baby daughter." His sarcasm cut through her heart. "So after years of searching for Susan, I finally found her. And now I have you, too."

Hannah's mind spun in a million different directions until dizziness threatened to overtake her. She wanted to sink down on the ground and just cry. No, she wanted to rush her biological father and clobber him. Not even that, she wanted to grab her birth mother and make a run for it.

Derek gripped her arm to hold her back. He must have sensed her confusion, but she knew she could never get close to that monster. She glanced at him to find a strange mixture of recognition and repulsion on his face.

She turned her attention back to the man who claimed to be her father. "Could I at least have your name?"

Her birth father shrugged. "Sure. Why not? This won't last long. I'm Sean O'Shea, and apparently I'm your real father."

Bile rose up in her throat at his words. "*Real* father? No way."

A look of venomous anger seized O'Shea's face. But in the man's distraction with Hannah, Derek whipped out his SIG Sauer and aimed it at the Mafia man. "Enough, O'Shea."

O'Shea looked at Derek and his weapon

and grinned, the anger gone. "Well. See? I knew you were our hero. Have you come to seek permission to court my daughter? How touching to see a polite, old-fashioned young man again. You're well-groomed, steady and serious enough, and you certainly know about self-defense. But one problem. You're a little too late."

"Too late for what?" Derek was rigid next to her, all muscles tensed and ready for a fight.

"You should have let her come alone rather than play the Good Samaritan. Now, you'll have to die as well. That's too bad. It looks like you could have had a promising career with whatever agency you're with."

O'Shea shoved her birth mother away, and she stumbled toward Hannah. Without thinking, Hannah pulled away from Derek and drew the woman in close. Derek followed until the three were huddled in a group.

O'Shea chuckled. "There's no chance here, hero boy. Three guns against one? Surely you knew I had a few associates with me." He turned his gaze on Hannah. "Now, I'm sorry that you won't be able to complete law school, but there's just too much at stake. Any questions you want to ask your father before we have to end this little family reunion?"

Hannah spoke through gritted teeth. "Like I said before, you're not my father. Willford McClarnon is my father." A gasp escaped. What would this monster do to him once he was done here?

"Willford. Rather hoity-toity, isn't it? But don't worry about him. He has nothing to contribute here, so he'll get to live. He'll live with the grief of the violent death of his beloved adopted daughter."

A sob escaped Hannah. How could she have come to this point in such a short period of time? Tears began to trickle down her cheeks in earnest. Tears that had been threatening to pour out all day.

Her birth father held out his arms, but his face contorted with malice. "Sweetheart, give me the doll, and we'll be done."

Her heart twisted at the idea of that man calling her a term of endearment. Worse yet, the doll? The handmade one? Hannah darted her gaze to Susan, who only looked at her, her face tearstained and forlorn. She pictured the doll nestled in her bag. That was what he wanted? "Why?"

"Susan told me all about it as we got reacquainted. I figured you would have gotten rid of it, and then I wouldn't have had to bother you. But I needed to make sure, to do my due diligence. Guess what I found online? Your little blog. That photo of all that stuff you called your *special keepsakes*. I know you have it. So, if you won't hand it over, do I have to go search the family home? I'm sure it's packed away there somewhere."

"Father?" The word escaped her lips, half in concern for her adoptive father and half a prayer to her heavenly Father.

"He may have raised you, but a DNA test would surely show that I'm dear old Dad." He gestured with his weapon. "You know what, though? It doesn't really matter, because only one of us is going to survive this little reunion." He eyed Derek, then Hannah, then Derek again. "Oh, I see another tragedy forming here today. Hero boy is sweet on you, Daughter. Too bad it won't come to anything, like…" He hummed a few bars of a popular wedding march.

Derek stood tall and looked her birth father in the eye. "You're right, Mr. O'Shea. I love her." His hand grasped hers. "I love Hannah. I've always loved Hannah. Not that it matters much, if you kill us all. But why don't you just let her go? She can't do anything to you, and then you'll just go back home and continue with your...*work*."

"Maybe you're not as bright as you seem, son. Either that, or you think I'm an idiot. You know what she knows. It's too much. She's no longer an asset to the family. She's a liability. And liabilities must be eliminated. Then I'll find what I'm looking for myself, starting at the family home."

He leveled his weapon at Hannah, the image of his gun blurred by her torrent of tears.

A drop of sweat trickled down Derek's temple, but he ignored it. "I don't think you really want to hurt her. So we're going to walk on out of here, and go back to our normal lives. Got it?" His adrenaline had spiked as he'd followed the SUV down the highway earlier. And when they had turned into the wooded park, he'd sped up. The remoteness and seclusion of the area had led him to speculate that the Mafia thugs would shoot Hannah and bury her in the woods. And now? Was that what was coming next if he couldn't get them out of there?

O'Shea moved his weapon to point at

Derek, exactly as Derek had wanted, although intense anger still twisted O'Shea's face. "Who do you think you are, hero boy? Giving me orders? And how could you possibly know what I want and don't want?"

If Derek could keep him talking, that could give Hannah and Susan a head start to get away. The pressure of the knowledge of who Sean O'Shea was, exactly, swarmed around him like a cloud of mosquitoes. When he had joined the FBI, he knew he wanted to fight organized crime. But he never imagined his first assignment would bring him face-to-face with a killer, and that that killer would be the biological father of the woman he loved. He glared at the Mafia hit man in front of him. "She's your daughter, O'Shea. Do you really want to do this?"

O'Shea threw his full attention at Derek. Slowly, an evil glint flickered in his eyes. "I have to."

Derek had no response but just gripped his SIG more tightly.

"Paralyzed with fear, boy? You should be." In his excitement, Hannah's birth father swung his weapon around in wild gesticulations.

As O'Shea continued his rant, stomping

around and raising little puffs of dust, Derek grabbed the opportunity. He raised his SIG and fired a shot, but in his nervousness, his hand wobbled at the pull of the trigger. The sound, like a loud firecracker, filled the woods. A rock the size of a soccer ball exploded a couple of feet away from O'Shea.

"Go!" He yelled to Hannah and Susan, gesturing to them to get behind a nearby boulder.

Fragments of rock flew across the clearing. Her birth father jumped into a crouch, looking around wildly for the rock shrapnel. Even though Derek hadn't hit his mark, for the moment, O'Shea's attention was off Derek and Hannah.

Suddenly, Derek had the few seconds he needed.

He followed Hannah and her birth mother toward the large boulder, pushing lightly on Hannah's back to urge her on. A bullet hit the boulder just as they dodged behind and into shelter.

"Keep going! Get to safety." He pointed to a narrow deer path through the trees in the direction of the parking lot. "Head that way. Get in the car. I'll catch up."

Hannah and her birth mother took off, pushing the slap of branches away from their faces and stumbling over downed trees. Derek whispered a quick prayer for their safety, then turned back to locate O'Shea and his henchmen.

He peered around the boulder. O'Shea and his thugs were on the other side of the clearing, seemingly searching among the thick trees and underbrush for the threesome. Before Derek could take off, the thug spotted him. He nudged his boss.

Derek's chest constricted, and he tightened his hold on his weapon. He wanted to glance back to see if Hannah and her mother were out of sight, but he didn't want to lose visual contact with O'Shea, either. Without the sound of the crunching of branches and the slapping of leaves and limbs from behind him, he could only assume that they were well on their way to safety.

In fact, an eerie silence filled the woods.

Sean O'Shea stared right at him, menace shining in his eyes. Slowly, he raised his weapon and pointed it at Derek.

His years of weapons training had not been in vain. Derek whipped his SIG up, trained it on the arm that held O'Shea's weapon, and shot it in the center.

Her birth father screamed out in pain as a large crack tore through the air.

O'Shea and his thugs ducked for cover. A searing pain ripped through Derek's bicep as he turned to run. He and O'Shea must have fired at the same time, and the man's bullet had caught him on the same arm. He touched the spot, suppressing a grimace of pain, and found fresh blood. There wasn't time to deal with that now. Hannah and Susan should be back at the vehicle, and he was desperate to join them and get them all to safety.

He dashed through the woods, dodging trees and leaping over rocks. In his haste, his own noise was so loud that he couldn't hear if anyone was following him. What seemed like too many minutes later, he broke free of the woods. Susan was huddled low in the backseat of the Cherokee. Hannah sat in the passenger seat. He heard the engine running as he drew closer.

A thick branch slapped him in the face and scraped across his cheek as he emerged through the tree line. A few seconds later, he was at the vehicle. Hannah leaned low over the driver's seat and pushed the door open. He slid in and threw the vehicle into Reverse. It chewed gravel as it fought for traction. Derek berated himself for not thinking of parking the vehicle in a position for an easy getaway, but there was nothing to do about that now. At least Hannah had found the keys he had left behind.

He pointed the SUV toward the driveway out to the road. In the rearview mirror, he spied Sean and his thugs burst from the woods, guns at the ready. Derek slid the SUV into Drive and hit the accelerator. "Get down!" He hunched over the steering wheel as Hannah and her mother slid down into their seats.

The thug fired off his weapon. Hannah covered her ears at the sound of the crack.

Derek surveyed the interior of the car, but no one was hurt and there didn't seem to be any damage. The bullet must have hit the back door.

As the vehicle surged forward, loose gravel from the parking area sprayed back onto O'Shea and his henchmen. They threw up their arms to shield their faces, and Derek turned onto the road without any more shots fired.

He settled into his seat and fastened his seat belt as he sped toward the park exit. Hannah and her birth mother seemed to relax into their seats, but Derek was certain they would soon be followed. The wound on his arm throbbed, but it didn't feel deep. He would get medical care as soon as he was certain of their safety, but there was no knowing when that would be.

He glanced over at Hannah, who wore a wide-eyed, tight-lipped look of panic on her face. "Are you all right? Not hurt?" He moved his eyes to the back to include Susan in his question.

"I'm okay," Hannah answered. She crossed her arms over her front, as if hugging herself.

Derek had a sudden longing to wrap her in his embrace, to whisper to her that she was safe and secure, to shield her from all of life's pain. What he had said was true. He did love her. But whether or not there could be any kind of lasting relationship was yet to be determined.

Susan sat silent in the backseat and just nodded. Living a life in fear had probably made her withdrawn and reluctant to open up. But the time would come soon when Hannah would want some answers.

He turned the Cherokee out of the park entrance and onto the state highway that would lead them back toward the city. A little down the road, though, he saw another vehicle, a dark sedan, turn out of the state park. Was it O'Shea and his goons? There were now a couple of cars between them, but they had been on the state highway already when Derek pulled out in front of them.

Now what? His mind raced with possible scenarios, none of them good. How much longer could they go on like this? It was gratifying to have saved Hannah's birth mother from a life-threatening situation. But now he had another person to protect. Another person to hide. Another reason Hannah's birth father and his associates would be after them. He needed to look at the situation realistically, of course, but a positive attitude would help as well.

Where could they go? Derek ran a hand roughshod over his hair. He was out of ideas. A fresh FBI Academy graduate on a case by himself? He should have known it was impossible. Sure, the Bureau had believed in him. They wouldn't have sent him otherwise. But the parameters of his assignment had been simple. Protect Hannah. And he'd let it get out of hand. He'd blazed in, confident of his abilities, and now he'd let everyone down. Including Hannah.

Especially Hannah.

There was no way to make this right.

He'd failed his parents, hiding out of fear for his own life instead of trying to save them. He could have done something—*anything*—to protect them. But he had cowered in terror as a thirteen-year-old boy. A shudder coursed through him at the memory of them lying dead on the ground, blood pooling, as he'd choked back petrified screams. Now, he was in the same position, against the Mafia again, and he was completely helpless. First, he had failed his mother and father. Now, he was failing the woman he loved.

ELEVEN

Hannah stared out the passenger-side window, worrying a cuticle on her finger. Should she keep a watch behind them, perhaps in her side mirror, to see if the bad guys were sneaking up on them? Or was that Derek's job? He was the one with both the rearview mirror and the law-enforcement training.

But with her heart pounding up into her throat and making it feel like her brain would explode with the pressure, she wasn't sure she could just sit back and relax.

In her first year of law school, her criminal law professor had given the class a tip that, at the time, had seemed superfluous. The stress of school then and a law practice after graduation would be tremendous, the professor had said, so it would be important to take some time for deep breathing. It was simple advice. Easy to remember. She had tucked it away in the deep recesses of her mind, fairly certain she wouldn't need it. But now? Now, it seemed incredibly helpful.

She stared straight out the front windshield and forced herself to close her eyes, trusting Derek to keep a lookout. She took several deep breaths, holding each while she counted to five.

There had been so much information to digest in such a short period of time. She was adopted. Her life had been in danger at the time of her adoption, and it was in danger again now. The letter and the handmade doll from her birth mother, who now sat huddled in the backseat. Her birth father was trying to kill her and probably her birth mother, too. No wonder she was overwhelmed.

Derek reached over and touched her arm. "We'll be fine."

She only nodded in response. She appreciated his reassurance, but the lines creasing around his eyes belied his own concern.

And what about her father, Willford McClarnon? She had spent a fair amount of time resenting him. He had held information from her deliberately. And yet, he had had his reasons. It was true that their social circles were rather snobby and judgmental. Her parents were completely right about that. They also had claimed they hadn't told her that she was adopted because they needed to protect her. She had been doubtful at first, but hadn't that protection proved to be a necessity? Trouble had still found her, but how much worse would it have been if she had gone digging for information years ago without Derek as her protector?

Whether or not she felt it in her heart at that moment, didn't she have an obligation, as a Christian, to forgive? No one ever said it would be easy, but God commanded it. That feeling of love and closeness may take a while to reach her heart. But at that moment, right then in that vehicle, she would choose God's way and forgive her father. It was a solid feeling that warmed her to her core.

Whether the decision not to tell her was right or wrong, she couldn't determine. But a review of the years she had spent with both her adoptive father and mother confirmed that they had loved her, and still did love her, wholeheartedly. A new appreciation for his love and care welled up in her, forcing a few tears to spring forth. She swiped them away with the back of her hand.

She opened her eyes and took one last deep

breath, turning to offer a reassuring smile to her birth mother. But Susan cowered against the far back door of the vehicle. She had drawn herself down and into the seat as much as possible, and a frightened look haunted her eyes. How long had she lived like this? Wherever she had been, she was good at hiding if it had taken all these years for O'Shea to find her.

Hannah's heart ached at the idea of a life of fear and constantly looking over her shoulder, and she reached out in between the front seats. Susan stretched out to gently clasp her hand for a brief moment, then shrank back against the door. Maybe, if they all lived long enough, there would be time for a relationship later.

For a moment, she watched her birth mother watch the scenery whiz past the window, and thanked God again for her adoptive parents and the solid upbringing they had given her. They had had their difficult moments, but no one was perfect. Only God was perfect, and He had known what He was doing when He gave her to Willford and Evelyn McClarnon.

And what about Derek? He'd proclaimed right there, in the heat of the moment, in the line of fire, in front of both of her birth parents, that he loved her. Was it true? She had thought, in high school, that he loved her, although he had never said it quite exactly like that. It seemed to be implied many times. But then he had left, and she thought she had been wrong. Maybe she *hadn't* been wrong. Or was it all a ruse to throw off her father and his intended attack? To take the attention off of her? Their kiss had been genuine, though, filled with emotion straight from their hearts.

She glanced at his profile, his strong jaw showing a determination that most wouldn't want to tangle with. Did she love him? Of course she did. She had loved him in the past, ready to confess it if he did first, although he never had. But their love for each other didn't mean that a relationship, a marriage, even, could work. His job didn't lend itself to a wife and family. And now everything had changed as well because she had knowledge that she had been adopted.

The side mirror showed a dark sedan approaching at a steady rate. A minivan was between them, but the sedan was definitely driving fast. Her heart thumped erratically in her chest. Was it them? She forced herself to look back out the front windshield. Derek was driving. He would know what to do.

A moment later, his hand enveloped hers. A heady warmth emanated up her arm and into her heart, giving her an extra dose of courage she didn't know she had. What did it mean, this affection? This touch? Just then, she wasn't sure she cared. She didn't have the stamina for any further examination of their relationship, or lack thereof. She simply closed her eyes, soaking up all the comfort and strength he was willing to send her way. And she prayed. Prayed to understand and accept.

Hannah felt the car jump forward as Derek hit the accelerator. Wherever that dark sedan was, apparently Derek wanted to get some distance between them. Maybe now was the time to ask her birth mother a few questions. She could gather some information and distract herself from the danger at hand.

"Susan?" Hannah turned toward the backseat and caught her mother's startled eye. "Is it all right if I call you Susan?"

The woman nodded.

"Can I ask you about our history together? What happened with my birth father, and why did you give me up for adoption?"

Susan stared out the window for several moments, and Hannah wondered if perhaps she wasn't willing to tell the story. But then she sighed heavily and turned her mournful gaze back to Hannah. "You know by now that your father is a part of a Mafia family."

Hannah nodded and waited for her to continue.

"I fell in love with him when I didn't know his family. I had no idea what he was. We met at the mall, hanging out at the video arcade with our friends. Before long, we were together all the time, behaving in ways we shouldn't have." Another sigh. "I know now that behavior was wrong. But it wasn't long, and I was pregnant. When I found out who his family was and what their so-called business was, I was horrified. But I was stuck. I was having his child and had no way to support myself, let alone a child, if I left him. As you probably know, it's not that easy to leave a Mafia family anyway." She chuckled, a sound of misery rather than mirth.

"I've heard." She glanced at Derek, who nodded his affirmation.

"So we got an apartment together. He always seemed to have a lot of money, which was fun. But he was also gone a lot, and he never talked about his work. I had no idea what he did in the hierarchy of the family."

"What did he think of your pregnancy?" Hannah's abdomen twisted at the notion that her own biological father didn't care if she was alive or dead, but she had to hear the answer.

"I don't know. He never talked about it. He didn't ever express excitement, but he gave me money for the doctor's appointments. Maybe if I'd stayed, he would have loved you."

It seemed clear what his intentions were now, and they didn't involve any kind of love. But Hannah didn't want her birth mother to feel any more guilt, so she kept silent. "Don't blame yourself. You did what you thought was best at the time."

"In the end, I didn't feel like I had any choice." She hugged her arms around her middle. "When you were not quite a year old, you toddled into our closet and got too curious about a fireproof safe that Sean normally kept locked. I had no idea what was in it and never thought about it much. But that day, you found it unlocked and pulled everything out before I found you. You were sitting on the floor in the closet, holding a leather-bound journal, flipping through the pages and happy as could be to see the paper turn."

"Was it something important?"

"I'll say. You'd found his kill log, the journal where he kept the details of the hits he'd carried out for the family. I don't know how I had the presence of mind, but I bundled you up and we ran to the copy store. I used their self-service copier and made a photocopy. At home, I tried to replace all the papers as they must have been, but I hadn't seen it before you pulled everything out."

Susan's eyes blazed as if she were reliving the panic. "Of course, he found out, probably when he got into the safe again and it wasn't arranged the same. Suddenly, I was rarely alone. The family began monitoring me closely, and I knew I needed to escape, especially with you. I wanted to protect you from your father and a life controlled by an organized crime syndicate." She sagged back into her seat and the light disappeared from her eyes, as if she was exhausted from telling the sequence of events.

Hannah turned a little more toward the back and spotted the dark sedan still following. It was closer, but she couldn't make out the people inside. She didn't have much time to get Susan to tell the rest. The poor woman looked tired of talking, but Hannah was determined to get as much information as she could before it was too late. "So what did you do?"

"I staged my own death. At least, that was my goal. I'd seen police shows and read books, and I just did the best I could at providing evidence. I chopped off some of my hair to leave in the car, and there ended up being blood in there as well. The blood was truly an accident. I set up my car to crash into a ditch. When I was jumping out of it as it went off the road, I scraped my head and my arm. Obviously, I never convinced Sean. He's a smart man. But at the time, I was away from him. And I've evaded him for more than twenty years."

"How did you manage all that with me in tow?" Hannah was amazed at her mother's ingenuity and her courage. Would she have been able to do the same? Thank the Lord she had never had to find out. Her gratitude for her easy and quiet life was growing exponentially.

"I had already given you to a lawyer who had found adoptive parents for you. Jumping out of the car as it went over the ditch may sound hard, but the most difficult thing I've ever had to do was give you up for adoption. I cried and cried. But I knew that was the best thing for you. It was better for you to live with adoptive parents than not to live at all." Susan closed her eyes, clearly exhausted from talking about the past.

Hannah whispered, "Thank you for telling me." She turned back to the front and caught Derek looking between her and the road. He raised his eyebrows and nodded at her as if to say that God had been looking out for her.

She ran a hand across her forehead and over her hair. He was right. God had protected her. He had led her to just the right family for her. Why she had merited this favor she didn't know, but gratitude swelled in her spirit.

"Do you know what happened to the doll I made for you?" Susan leaned forward and touched Hannah hesitantly on the shoulder.

The doll. Hannah felt as if her brain spasmed as she remembered O'Shea asking about the doll. "Yes, it's here." She pulled her bag open and dug around until she found it.

"Have you found what I hid inside?"

"Inside the doll? No." She squeezed and squished it in both hands. A lump in the middle urged her to retrieve her fingernail scissors from her purse. She snipped open the back seam.

Her birth mother peered over the seat, observing the procedure, and Derek bounced his gaze from the road ahead to the rearview mirror to the doll's impromptu surgery. "Is it still there?" Susan asked.

Hannah dug in to the doll and pulled out a roll of half sheets of paper. She opened them to find them covered with handwritten notes.

"That's it!" Hannah turned to see her birth mother smile for the first time. "You have it. That's the copy I made of his log."

A grim smile stretched across Derek's face. "Quickly, take photos with your phone and send them to my supervisor. No matter what happens, we'll have a copy then."

Hannah snapped the pictures and forwarded them to the address Derek recited.

They had real evidence now and that was something, even if they didn't yet have the man behind it all.

A breath of relief stuck in her throat and morphed to fear as Derek leaned over and whispered, "We have a tail."

She peered in the side mirror. Only one car separated them from the dark sedan now, and she squinted to see that Sean O'Shea was in the passenger seat. A claw seemed to grab her insides, and she clutched the armrest. "What do we do?"

"We keep driving." Derek ground his jaw in a way that oddly comforted Hannah.

But they couldn't drive in the Cherokee forever. At some point, they would have to deal with O'Shea and his goons. They would have to see it through. No matter what. Whatever would come, Hannah knew that Derek would jump into the line of fire for her. In the meantime, she would pray for God's grace.

Traffic had increased as the highway expanded to four lanes, and Derek wove in and out around trucks and large SUVs until he had left the dark sedan far enough behind that he couldn't see it in the rearview mirror any longer. He exhaled heavily, although he knew he couldn't relax for long. A guy like Sean O'Shea wouldn't give up and just let them go.

Still, something needed to be done. They needed a destination. A safe haven.

Something Susan had said to Hannah rang through his mind, and he couldn't eradicate it. *It was better for you to live with adoptive parents than not to live at all.* Was that why

God had spared him from the gun of his parents' killer when he was thirteen years old? After witnessing his parents' brutal murders, there had been many nights when he wished he had been killed as well. He had been angry with God for so long. His parents had been devout Christians. Why did they have to die? His aunt and uncle had been difficult and unaccepting of him, which made his high school years tumultuous, to say the least. Hannah had been the only bright beacon in his life.

But then he'd been forced to leave her. He probably would have done harm to himself if not for the part-time job he'd found in college. The campus minister hired him to sweep the office and take out the trash. They were odd jobs without much pay, but the man was kind and encouraging. Derek had been desperate for some encouragement. Soon, he began finding books left for him to read and sermon notes lying on the desk. He finally succumbed to the call of his spirit. His first time back in church since his parents' deaths, he's found himself on his knees, asking Jesus to lead his life.

Had God thought it was better for him to live?

The images of the murders and the cries of

his parents still haunted him. Recurring images made him doubt, every day, his ability to do his job. To protect Hannah. Would the FBI training fail him? Fail her? He gripped the steering wheel and swerved to another lane. But the FBI wouldn't have admitted him to the academy if they'd had any doubts about his ability. Many had dropped out in the five months of training, but he had stayed the course. He must have the chops to do the job. Was this why his life was spared? To protect and to help people through his position with the FBI?

He would have to ponder all that later. Right now, he had one task, and he needed to keep his focus on the end goal—figuring out how to keep Hannah and her birth mother safe from harm. The Mafia thugs couldn't be far behind and time was running out. They had to act fast.

He swallowed hard. "Hannah, I'm going to need some help."

She turned to him, her delicate brows arched above her soft, brown eyes.

If they survived this, could there be a future for them? *Stop it. Don't go there.*

"We need someplace to hide, and I'm fresh

out of ideas." Perhaps a team approach would be best.

She tapped her finger to her lips for a moment of silence. "What if it involves my parents?"

"Whatever keeps you safe." He wasn't eager to see Mr. McClarnon again, not after the episode in high school and then whisking his daughter away in a hail of gunfire while local police descended on his home. But if this was what Hannah thought best, he would trust her judgment.

"When Father and Mother built the new house, after moving the factory, Father had a secret room built into it. There's a panel behind a mirror in their bedroom. It's not very big, but from the outside, no one can tell that it's there."

"Like a vault?" Leave it to Mr. McClarnon to come up with something like that. There was a reason his business had grown to phenomenal proportions.

"Sort of. Wealthy men often build secret rooms as a security feature. For cash, bonds, weapons, whatever."

"What if we head there?"

"I'll make the call." Hannah tapped her parents' number from her favorites list.

He nodded to the phone as she moved it to her ear. "Put it on speaker."

"Hannah." Mr. McClarnon's commanding voice filled the vehicle. "How are you? Are you safe? Are you well?"

"Father, you're on speaker. We're all right. I'm with Derek."

Derek quirked an eyebrow at her. Apparently, she didn't think it necessary to tell him about Susan just then. That discussion was probably best left for another time.

"Derek?"

He sat up straighter, as if facing the man himself. "Yes, sir."

"I'm glad I have the chance to speak with you."

Mr. McClarnon was always in charge of any conversation, and apparently, they weren't going to be given the opportunity to tell him what had happened since they last saw him or that they needed a safe house. Derek felt beads of perspiration break out on his forehead. Did this conversation have to happen right this instant? He was driving a vehicle and trying to evade the bad guys. How could he concentrate?

"I want to apologize to you, son."

Derek almost hit the brake in his surprise.

"To me, sir?" Had Mr. McClarnon just called him *son*, or had he imagined it?

"Yes. My words and attitude earlier were inappropriate and uncalled for. You have kept my little girl safe, and I appreciate it."

Derek's lips felt numb, but he mumbled, "Yes, sir."

"I know everyone says it, but it's true. You don't realize what you have until you might lose it. My girl is more important than any social standing or what others might think. Thank you for protecting her. If you can find some time to stop by, I'd like to start fresh. Apologize in person. Ask your forgiveness. Talk about your relationship with Hannah."

Hannah stared at him, and he forced himself to look back at the road. "Um, that's wonderful, sir. How about now?" The tires squealed as he changed lanes again on the four-lane highway. A mile marker whizzed by, but he couldn't catch the number.

"Sure." Surprise tinged the man's voice, something Derek hadn't heard before. "I'll be here."

"I'd say we'll be there in about fifteen minutes."

After Hannah ended the call, Derek quickly called his supervisor. A plan was forming in his mind. Perhaps it would be feasible to catch Sean O'Shea, Mafia hit man, and also complete his assignment of keeping Hannah safe. His supervisor confirmed that backup would be on the way. But Derek and Hannah would arrive first at the McClarnon house and hide in safety, assuming the secretive and always-in-control Mr. McClarnon even acknowledged the existence of his safe room.

TWELVE

Hannah's old bedroom and private bathroom called to her as Derek drove the Cherokee into the open garage and hopped out to close the door behind them. She wanted nothing more than a hot bath and a fresh change of clothes, but that was going to have to wait.

They breezed past her parents' butler, making excuses for what must seem to him to be rude behavior, all the while urging him to gather the staff in a safe place. Her parents were in the library, an afternoon tea laid out on the side table.

"Darling." Her mother stepped forward for an embrace and a kiss on the cheek.

Hannah obliged eagerly, but she must have approached with too much force for her mother steadied herself with a step back. "I'm sorry, Mother. We're in a bit of a rush."

She stepped toward her father and kissed

his cheek. "I'm sorry, Father, if I've seemed ungrateful or rebellious. I do appreciate all we have here."

"No, darling, you've done nothing wrong. I should have allowed you more freedom."

"I understand why, though, now. A law career will take me places where I could be in danger, especially if I should pursue criminal law or any field that would bring me into contact with the Mafia. You thought it was safest to stay here."

"There is more you will want to hear."

Derek cleared his throat and stepped forward. "Sir? If we could get to that secret room?"

He gazed at Derek as if seeing him for the first time. "Yes. Of course."

Hannah linked arms with her mother. "Perhaps you could tell me on the way."

For the first time, the McClarnons noticed Susan, who stood as much behind Hannah as she could manage. Hannah, kicking herself for forgetting her manners in the difficult situation, pulled her birth mother forward and introduced her to her adoptive parents. Her mother embraced Susan, and her father shook her hand with a gentle smile, but Derek suggested they would have time to get to know each other later.

Her father led the way out of the library as her mother walked by her side. "It started with a phone call from an old family friend, a lawyer who went to university with your father. He said that he had a little girl in need of a home and asked if we would know anyone who wanted to adopt. He seemed desperate, and even though that didn't typically happen in our circles, we said we would ask around."

Derek brought up the rear, his hand on his weapon. His vigilance was nearly palpable, and Hannah forced herself to concentrate on her mother. "I was the little girl?"

"Yes, and we couldn't get you out of our minds. We talked about it late into the night, and by the next morning, we were sure that this was a child God had sent to us. Your brother was about three years old, and it had only been a month prior that the doctor had told me that I would never be able to have more children." Her voice caught and she took a moment to collect herself before going on. "We were elated to know we were going to bring home a little girl. But you remember what we said before. We also had the challenge of how to tell your father's business associates and our society friends. " Her mother pulled an embroidered handkerchief from her skirt pocket and dabbed some moisture from her cheeks.

As her father led the group down the hallway, he turned around with a wry grin. "In hindsight, they don't fit the definition of true friends, now, do they?"

Hannah felt a squeeze on her shoulder. It was Derek from behind, offering a silent but comforting gesture.

"So we invented a trip," her mother continued in a steady voice, "to hide the fact that I wasn't really pregnant. We rented a small condo in a Chicago suburb to collect you and get to know you before we returned and to wait out the rest of my pretend pregnancy. I'm sorry for the pretense, and I regret it now. But we didn't know what else to do. I told a few friends and let the news out that I was pregnant. I told everyone I was about seven months along."

"Seven months? And they believed you?"

"I told them the baby was small. We said that your father was being transferred away for a six-month assignment. When we got you, we were thrilled. You were so cuddly and adorable, with chubby little legs and silky strands of blond hair. It was love at first sight. But you were older than we had expected. Quite a bit older. Our friends were expecting us to bring home a newborn but you were already a year old."

Hannah patted her adoptive mother's arm as they turned the corner into the bedroom. She could see the large gilt mirror her mother had checked her hair in just the day before.

"As it turned out, I had told the truth about the baby being small. You were small for your age. Healthy, according to the doctor, but small. But it was still going to cause questions. So your father returned to our home a couple of times to put out the word that his assignment had been extended while your brother and you stayed in Chicago with me."

Her father revealed a small panel in a writing desk and pushed a couple of buttons. The large mirror slowly slid to the side. A panel with a finger hold at one side filled the space behind it. "I had plant managers who ran the operation here, and I kept in touch with them by phone and facsimile. No one questioned me, but then they wouldn't have had the courage."

Her mother embraced her as they stopped outside the panel. "Oh, darling. We wanted to tell you so many times. To cast aside the expectations of your father's business partners and our social circle, especially after adoption became more socially acceptable. But somehow, it seemed too big to talk about. And we were still gravely concerned with your safety. We never forgot the warning."

Derek pulled the panel open and whistled when he saw the large safe and the gun rack hidden inside. Hannah glanced at him, but her father drew her attention from the inside of the room that she had never seen before.

"Hannah, would you forgive us?" Moisture dampened her father's eyes.

She could only nod as Derek, with a hand on the small of her back, urged her into the safe room.

Mr. McClarnon leaned in to speak low. "It's a one-way mirror, so you'll be able to see out and into the bedroom."

"What do you mean, sir?" Derek puffed the front of his shirt to get some air. "You're coming in with us. You two and Susan."

Hannah gripped his arm from behind. Her anxiety over the safety of her parents radiated through her touch.

"No. We'll stay out here and be your front

guard." Mr. McClarnon put a firm grip on Derek's forearm. "Son, I command an entire company. I know you're the FBI agent, but your job is to protect my daughter. I appreciate your concern for us, but I'm staying out here. I'm protecting my daughter, too." He pointed Susan farther into the bedroom. "There's a dressing room and closet suite where you can hide. You'll be safest there, since they'll have to come through us first."

Derek could only nod, a lump in his throat. Hannah's father, the one who had destroyed all hope of a relationship with his daughter years ago, had just called him *son*. Again. He hadn't heard that term of endearment for over a decade. Did it mean anything? He shook his head to clear his thoughts. There wasn't opportunity to analyze it now. Lives were on the line, and it was his responsibility to make sure they all survived.

The air-conditioning kicked on, and he felt a cool draft rush down from the ceiling in the walk-in safe. At least they would have fresh air.

"This is not a safe room, per se. It's not bullet-proof. It's simply a hidden room to stash valuables." He scrubbed a hand across his face. "I never thought it would be used to hide human valuables."

"What about a weapon for you, sir?"

"I have a handgun in the bedside table."

"Shooting isn't always best. Do you have anything of any weight that you could throw or distract the bad guys with?"

"A fire extinguisher under the bed, for emergencies."

"Good. Keep that handy, and watch me for a signal if needed. Backup is on the way. Pray they get here first."

Derek nodded to Mr. McClarnon, who went to stand next to his wife, who was already perched on the edge of a chair. Susan was out of sight. Then he stepped inside the safe and pushed the button on the wall to slide the panel shut. Hannah stepped up next to him and linked her arm through his. They stared through the mirror for a moment, watching her parents talk.

As much as he enjoyed the fact that Hannah had come to lean on him for strength and support, she hadn't given any indication that she returned his affection. His feelings were stronger now than ever, but perhaps he needed to be prepared to walk away when it was all over no matter how much he disliked that notion. He withdrew his arm from hers and looked around the small space. The walls were covered with built-in cabinets, presumably filled with the McClarnon valuables. An air duct blew cool air from the ceiling. But that was it. No other door or even a space that could fit an adult.

"Well, there's no escape here. No secret tunnel. No getting out except back through the looking glass." He attempted a smile, but it felt like it never made it to his face.

"As my father mentioned, it wasn't meant to hide people. But at least we have air." Her facial muscles twitched, but a smile never reached her lips. "And now we just wait for the cavalry to arrive?"

"Yes, and it shouldn't be long." He glanced out at Mr. and Mrs. McClarnon, darkened by the mirror. "You have some pretty terrific parents."

A contemplative look settled on Hannah's beautiful face. "Yes, they are. But…"

"But what? It's obvious how much they love you."

"I know how blessed I am to have them in my life. I just wish they had told me from the beginning that I was adopted. But they had good reason not to. I understand that."

"Humans are fallible, Hannah. No one is perfect. But the Lord is perfect, and He has adopted us as His sons and daughters." He ran a hand through his hair, trying to calm his jitters. "It's the ultimate adoption, taking us as His own. He doesn't tell us everything, either, but we know that He does what is best for us."

As she mulled that over, he touched his weapon in the holster, an almost subconscious gesture. He glanced back at her to see that a smile had erupted on her face. "You're right." She looked out the mirror at her mother and father. "If we get out of this alive—"

"No *if*s. We *are*." He watched Mr. and Mrs. McClarnon hold hands as he stood next to her outside the mirror. Mr. McClarnon had retrieved his handgun and held it in his free hand. The fire extinguisher sat on the floor behind the chair. It wouldn't be long and this would all be over, and he would move on to another assignment.

"Hannah, I'm not sure what's going to happen after this, but I want you to know how sorry I am for how things turned out in high school. I'm not a rebellious person, and I didn't want to defy your father. But I could have at least said goodbye." Just like he would have to say goodbye again. Soon.

Moisture glistened in her eyes. "I understand, Derek. I wish a lot of things could have been different, but here we are, and we need to make the best of it. Besides, I only have a year left of law school, and then I know my family has a lot of charities that could use some legal help. I'll be busy. You'll be on to another job, and you'll be busy. We'll be fine."

Fine? No, they wouldn't be fine. They would be living separate lives.

"Hannah, I don't want to say goodbye again. I love you, just like I've always loved you. Do you think—?"

A loud thud from a distant part of the house interrupted him, and he removed his SIG from the holster.

Hannah stared at him with wide brown eyes. "Are they here?"

"Probably. Get behind me."

"Is it the good guys or the bad guys?"

"We'll find out in a minute."

An instant later, a snarling Sean O'Shea with a couple of henchmen on his heels stormed into the bedroom. Their guns were pointed at Mr. McClarnon before he could even raise his.

Inside the safe, Derek raised his weapon and pointed it at O'Shea. He was prepared to shoot through the mirror if he had to, to save the McClarnons.

"Where are they? Show me. Now!" O'Shea's voice came through the mirror in a loud, clear tone.

Hannah grasped Derek's arm from behind and stifled her gasps in his shirt. The sound of her sobbing surrounded him. O'Shea stood still and looked around the room, his head cocked as if he was listening.

Derek froze. Hannah must have seen O'Shea from behind Derek, for a loud gasp erupted from her.

O'Shea's gaze settled on the mirror. He pointed his weapon at it.

His chest constricting, Derek jumped to the side of the mirror, pulling Hannah along with him. He turned his face and chest toward the wall and, with one smooth sweep of his arm, turned Hannah to face the wall as well, covering her with his body.

O'Shea shot at the mirror, the bullet lodging in the rear wall and pieces of mirror spraying everywhere.

A thousand pinpricks of pain sprayed across his back, but he didn't move. Hannah stood still, and he prayed she was protected from the bits of glass.

"Stay here." He kept his voice low and stepped away from the wall.

Hannah shrunk against the wall as if she wished she could be absorbed into it.

Derek locked eyes with Mr. McClarnon and tipped his head ever so slightly toward the fire extinguisher. Then he swung his gaze toward the middle of the room, looking at the floor in front of O'Shea and his guys. It wouldn't matter if Mr. McClarnon understood the signal if Derek couldn't get the bad guys' attention. They wouldn't hesitate to shoot him if they saw what Derek wanted him to do.

"We're here." He stepped into the opening where the mirror had been. "And we have the doll."

"Perfect." O'Shea took a step forward. "But first, hand over your weapon."

Derek shuffled to the side to give O'Shea the illusion that he was coming forward, and raised his SIG as if he was going to hand it over. But he cut his eyes at Mr. McClarnon and tipped his head toward O'Shea.

With all three intruders focused on Derek's

supposed surrender, Mr. McClarnon turned and grabbed the fire extinguisher from behind the chair. "Here!" he yelled as he lobbed it toward O'Shea. It landed at their feet.

With one smooth motion, Derek raised his SIG and fired one shot at the fire extinguisher. Mr. McClarnon turned his back to it to protect his wife in the chair. With his free arm, Derek reached behind to push Hannah farther into the safe. As soon as he saw his bullet had met its mark, he spun around to protect his face.

The fire extinguisher exploded, the force pushing O'Shea and his thugs against the wall. A stream of white powder shot toward them and spread through the room. It enveloped O'Shea and his men as they dropped their weapons to grab their eyes, choking and coughing in pain and surprise.

A few moments later, the cloud began to dissipate. Derek held the hem of his shirt to his face and pulled Hannah's up to her face. With O'Shea coughing violently, Derek rushed out to retrieve their weapons. As the chemicals penetrated the shirt and he began to cough, the room filled with FBI agents in Kevlar vests.

"It's over." He turned back to Hannah and

pulled her forward to see O'Shea and his thugs in handcuffs, lying on the carpet.

He grabbed her hand and pulled her out of the safe. "Let's go!" he called to the McClarnons. They rushed through the hallways and out to the veranda. Derek gulped the clean air, filling his lungs with fresh oxygen.

Mrs. McClarnon rushed to the outdoor sofa and sat down, with Mr. McClarnon right by her side.

"Is everyone all right? We're out of danger, so breathe deeply and clear your lungs. The agents inside will handle everything, and a medic will check us out soon."

Hannah stood shakily next to him, seemingly reluctant to reach out to him. Mr. McClarnon stood and shook Derek's hand. "Thank you, son." Then without breaking eye contact with Derek, he nodded toward Hannah.

Derek raised his eyebrows. He thought he knew what Mr. McClarnon meant, but he also knew it was more than he had dared to hope for. Could it be?

Then, Hannah's father said three simple words that changed his life forever. "I was wrong." And then two more. "Ask her."

Derek turned to Hannah. A smile stretched across her beautiful face even as tears coursed down her cheeks. As he had been wanting to do since their reunion, he gathered her in his arms. The gentleness of her arms around him erased all thought of the pain from his arm. "We got interrupted in there. In the safe room. So let me say it again." He ran a finger down her chin and thumbed away a tear. "I love you, Hannah. I always have. I always will."

Hannah glanced at her father then back at him. Uncertainty flitted across her face, but it was quickly replaced with understanding, relief. Joy. "I love you, too, Derek."

He stared down into her eyes, which shone with love for him. His mind reeled at what was happening, at this most incredible conclusion to their secret high-school romance and then ten years of separation. "Marry me?" As his lips brushed against hers, love exploded in his chest.

One last word from Hannah made his life complete. "Yes."

He was hers, and she was his. He could barely absorb it all, but now he had the rest of his life to live a dream come true.

"I'm here," he murmured in her hair, "now and forever."

EPILOGUE

Three months later, warm afternoon sun slanted across the McClarnons' spacious backyard and seeped into the edges of the large tent. Hannah fluffed the long, ruffled skirt of her wedding gown. Delicate pink rose buds adorned every table, and a similar pink rose was pinned to Derek's lapel, a striking contrast to the dark black of his tuxedo.

In another week, their lives would be thrown into chaos, as Hannah returned to law school for her final year and Derek traveled to Quantico for a week of catch-up and meetings. Hannah straightened her husband's boutonniere and rose to her tiptoes for a kiss. But for now, she would savor the moment.

"May I have your attention, please?" The murmurs of the large crowd dissipated at the wedding planner's announcement. "At this time, Mr. and Mrs. Chambers will cut the cake."

Hannah had to admit that she had never been a girl who dreamed of her wedding. But this was the stuff of fairy tales. Ruffles and lace and roses and a handsome man in a tuxedo who loved her and was willing to give his life for her.

A man who, at this moment, was holding a piece of cake up to her, ready to stuff it in her mouth.

Politeness reigned, and Derek held it still so she could take a nibble. As the sweet goodness melted in her mouth, she prayed that her marriage would be the same. A sweetness and goodness with Derek until death parted them.

Derek put down the plate and pulled her aside as servers began passing out the wedding cake to the guests. She leaned in close and savored the scent of his spicy aftershave, which mingled with the aroma of the flowers. "I love you," he murmured in her ear.

"Did you ever think we'd make it to this day?" Many times, in the years they had been apart, Hannah had cried into her pillow. She had been willing to live single and alone, but in that part of her spirit she didn't like to examine, she knew she didn't want to.

"After that meeting with your father when we were in high school, I never thought I'd see you again. I guess we can thank the FBI for all of this."

"Yes, and thank them for a promising future...for us both." A bridesmaid spotted her and smiled. Hannah smiled back, a stretch in her cheeks that was beginning to feel natural.

Derek ran a finger along her chin. "It was generous of them to transfer me to Indianapolis so soon after completing the academy."

"And a job for me upon graduation? I can't wait."

"They might move us again. There's no guarantee we'll stay here."

"I don't care where we go, as long as we're together."

She sipped her sparkling grape juice and surveyed the crowd, Derek's arm around her waist in a natural fit. Her birth mother, Susan, was chatting with her parents, and a smile popped out every now and then in the conversation. Her heart warmed at the idea of Mother and Father embracing her birth mother. Hannah, too, was getting to know her. Their relationship would never be the same as the one Hannah had with her adoptive mother, but it was growing and she was grateful.

"Have you had any news on Sean O'Shea?" The shock at her discovery that her birth father was a Mafia hit man who had wanted her dead still lingered. She could never call him her father. But forgiveness was slowly radiating through her heart.

"Nothing more. He's still in prison, awaiting trial. The prosecutor says he has a strong case, and it seems your birth mother will get justice. He won't be able to hurt any more families. Are you sure you want to think about that now?"

"It's just a question. I was thinking that I ought to visit him. Maybe get involved in prison ministry."

"Get to know him a little?"

"He'll never be a father to me, but yes."

"Speaking of fathers, your father seems to have accepted me."

Hannah gestured around her, encompassing the wedding reception tent, the guests and Derek in his tuxedo. "You think?" She smiled at him.

He smiled back, his dimples beckoning her in for another kiss. "Seriously. He's become the father I've missed since I was thirteen."

"I think his faith is growing as well. Mother told me they've had some strife from the country-club set. But Father is handling it well. He increasingly doesn't care what others think as long as he's in God's will."

The tinkling of tiny bells interrupted them, and Derek grinned at her in that charming way of his that always made her melt.

As their lips touched, a connection flitting between their spirits, Hannah looked forward to a joyous future with her soul mate by her side.

* * * * *

*If you enjoyed DEADLY DISCLOSURE,
look for UNDER DURESS
by Meghan Carver.*

Dear Reader,

What a thrill it is to present this second novel to you! The idea for this story came to me the day I noticed the discrepancy in dates on my own birth certificate. Unlike Hannah, I've always known I was adopted. Also unlike Hannah, my birth father was not in a Mafia family, but it was an interesting scenario to plot! With the danger following Hannah as a result of her adoption, I knew she would need someone familiar by her side. Derek from *Under Duress* seemed the perfect choice.

The ultimate theme of the story, though, for both Hannah and Derek, is adoption into the family of God. Hannah is shocked to learn that she was adopted, and she questions her entire life. But Derek, having struggled with his faith in his own circumstances and come out victorious, is there to remind her that all believers are adopted…into the family of God. Romans 8:15 tells us that we can approach our Heavenly Father without fear but with love and confidence. What a blessed assurance!

I would be honored to hear from you. You can visit my website at www.meghancarver. com, where you can sign up for my author newsletter, or email me at MeghanCCarver@ gmail.com. If you're on Facebook, I'd like to be your friend at Facebook.com/meghancarver. If you wish to write on good old-fashioned stationery, you can send it to me c/o Love Inspired Books, 195 Broadway, 24th Floor, New York, NY 10007.

Many blessings to you,
Meghan Carver

Get 2 Free Books,
Plus 2 Free Gifts—
just for trying the Reader Service!

LI17R2

Get 2 Free Books,
Plus 2 Free Gifts—
just for trying the Reader Service!

HOMETOWN HEARTS ♥

READERSERVICE.COM

Manage your account online!

- Review your order history
- Manage your payments
- Update your address

> *We've designed the*
> *Reader Service website*
> *just for you.*

Enjoy all the features!

- Discover new series available to you, and read excerpts from any series.
- Respond to mailings and special monthly offers.
- Browse the Bonus Bucks catalog and online-only exculsives.
- Share your feedback.

Visit us at:

ReaderService.com